ICICLE DREAMS

Mistletoe Meadows
Book 2

JESSIE GUSSMAN

Contents

Acknowledgments

Cover art by Covers and Cupcakes
Editing by Heather Hayden
Narration by Jay Dyess
Author Services by CE Author Assistant

Listen to the unabridged audio for FREE performed by Jay Dyess on the Say with Jay channel on YouTube. Get early access to all of Jay's recordings and listen to Jessie's books before they're available to the general public, plus get daily Bible readings by Jay and bonus scenes by becoming a Say with Jay channel member.

Chapter One

*A*my McBride scooped dog food out of the bin. She tried not to sigh at the sight of the bottom of the bin as she picked her scoop up.

There was enough left for maybe two days. Three, if the two dogs that were being boarded went home today. And if she was very, very careful.

Dog food had increased in price dramatically over the last four years, and she did not have enough money in her account for even one bag.

All she had in her own cupboard were dried beans and a few bags of rice along with some pasta and some cans of tomatoes. She didn't even have sauce.

Lord, I know I'm not supposed to worry, but I feel like You're cutting it a little close.

Immediately she felt bad. Her tone was not humble or respectful.

I'm sorry, Lord. You know best. If I'm supposed to keep these dogs, You need to provide for them. And if I'm not, please help me to figure out what to do with them before we all starve.

There. That was a little better. She really did believe God was in control and that God planned things, and she absolutely believed with all of her heart and soul that God had wanted her to open up this pet sanctuary.

But when they had lost the Richmond Rebel sponsorship because she had trained someone who opened a pet sanctuary closer to their garage, she'd been struggling.

She didn't regret training Nolita to open up her own place, and she didn't begrudge Nolita the funding that came with the Richmond Rebels. In fact, Blade Truax, one of the brothers who owned the garage, had specifically talked to her about it. She had told him it was fine. She had wanted Nolita to have as much funding as possible and the best chance of success. She didn't want to be selfish.

But looking back, she wished she would have been just a little bit selfish. Although she figured even with the funding, Nolita was probably struggling the same way she typically did. There were so many animals and only so much money to go around.

Mocha shoved her nose through the wires as Amy poured dog food in the automatic feeder.

None of the automatic feeders were full. She was just putting in enough for one daily ration. She had checked the rations carefully and measured them out just as carefully. She wasn't going to give one ounce more than what she had to, but she wanted all the dogs to have what they needed.

"You're a sweetheart," she said to Mocha. The little dog was so affectionate. Even though her food was ready for her to eat, and she hadn't had anything extra in days, she still wanted to stay and have Amy pet her. She was some kind of terrier mixed with a large breed dog, which made her about fifty pounds, and all sweetness and affection. Mocha would make an amazing house pet for someone, but typically around the holidays, pet adoptions went down.

"You'll probably spend Christmas with me, which...it's not so bad, is it?" she asked, knowing that while she'd spend some time with the dogs, she'd also be with her family, her mom and her five siblings. They were all supposed to be in for Christmas, and there might even be some extra since she was fairly certain that her sister Terry would be bringing her... She didn't say that he was her boyfriend, but Judd was going to have that title, or even fiancé, soon.

She smiled, the idea of Terry being happy making her happy. Terry had been an example to her all throughout her life. Growing up, she could look to Terry to know what she should do. Humans were hardwired to have examples to look at and to emulate, to follow. So many of her classmates followed whatever it was on their TV, but Amy had been blessed. She had Terry.

Moving to the next dog, she scooped out of the bucket she carried and measured carefully.

Boomer came to the wire and stuck his nose through, waiting anxiously for his breakfast.

"Hey, Boomer. What's going on with you this morning?" she said as she scratched his ears while she poured the food in his automatic feeder.

He whined, and instead of going right over to his food like he typically did, he licked her hand.

The action made tears prick her eyes. He was so trusting. It was almost like he could tell that there was something on her mind. Something she worried about, and he wanted to make it better.

"I'm just going to trust God, Boomer. It's going to be okay."

She knew her words were true, but she also figured that if dogs could sense anxiety, they were probably sensing it in her right now. As much as she was trying to have faith and trust that God would take care of everything.

The dog licked her hand one more time and whined before going over and starting to eat his food.

She blinked back tears. She would figure something out. She had already been working part-time in her friend Jones's veterinary clinic. She manned the desk when he needed it and worked with him as a vet tech, either on farm calls or in his practice. He was mostly a small animal vet, but when a farmer around Mistletoe Meadows called an emergency, Jones did not turn them down.

His practice was not big. His "clinic" was in an elderly couple's garage, and he lived over the top. It was very unassuming, but that was Jones. He wanted to get his school bills paid off and a clientele established before he got his own building and sank a bunch of money into it.

She thought that was smart, and she knew that he was using everything that he made to try to pay his bills back after paying rent.

Regardless, she hadn't made enough to supplement what she lost when she lost the funding, and she was slowly sinking down into the red to the point where she was going to have to close. Or do something drastic; she wasn't sure what.

She emptied the last of the food in the bucket into the next dog's feeder and went back to fill up the bucket again. As she scraped the dog food from the bottom of the barrel, she thought about Elisha and the widow with the cruse of oil.

Was this how she felt? Almost running out, only it wasn't animals that were going to die with her, it was her son. That had to be worse.

Amy knew that she could always move in with her mom, but her mom already had her brother Gilbert, whose wife was dying of cancer, and their three children living there, and her younger sister Isadora was possibly moving in as well. Her husband had decided that he didn't love her anymore and had found someone else, and had left. He had not been kind when he had done it, and Isadora, who had been a stay-at-home mom, had been crushed.

Amy had wanted to go and strangle her ex, but obviously that wasn't the Christian thing to do. Still, it made her mad that someone could say vows, have a family, set up a home, and then just decide they didn't want to anymore.

That showed such a lack of character. Such a lack of decency. She just didn't understand it.

Well, in a way she did. She understood that human desires often affected human decisions. It was true for her.

Maybe that was why she was struggling so much. Maybe it hadn't been God's will for her to open this after all. Maybe she had just desired it so much that she had superimposed what she wanted as God's will.

She'd seen people do that, excuse their sin, saying it was God's will. She'd even seen a man, an assistant pastor, who cheated on his wife and left her and said that the woman that he left her for was God's will for him.

Her jaw dropped open when she heard that, but how did she argue with someone who was blind? She could point out black-and-white in the Bible that adultery was wrong. That breaking his word was wrong. That lying was wrong. Making promises that he didn't keep was wrong. That a man was supposed to provide for his family. And to not do so was wrong.

She just didn't understand it. At least she hadn't sinned, to her knowledge, in opening her pet sanctuary.

Just because things are hard, it doesn't mean you should doubt God.

Wow. That was the thought that she needed. It was funny how those things popped into her head at the most random times. Things she might have heard in a sermon or read in the Bible, and then, when she most needed them, they popped into her mind, or she should probably give credit where it was due and say that God brought it to mind.

Carrying the bucket back, hunching her shoulders against the cold December wind, she walked back to the shelter where the front pens were. Each pen had an outside run, and all of those would need to be cleaned this morning as well.

At least it wasn't below freezing. Where the dog poop froze before she could get it off the ground and then it just piled up until the ground finally unfroze and she had a huge mess.

Rain made things muddy and messy as well, and she was thankful that it was just cold and not miserable.

"Here you go, Alice. You thought I forgot about you." She dumped dog food into Alice's pan and patted the furry head before walking on.

Her brother Wilson and his friend, her sister's almost-boyfriend, had just put up a whole side of new pens for her. She already had dogs in them, two of which were boarders, and she would be getting money for their stay, thankfully. It couldn't come soon enough.

If you just told someone, you know a lot of people who would love to help you.

She sighed as she petted another wet nose and scooped more dog food out.

She didn't want to burden her friends and family even more. When she lost the funding, she'd mentioned to them that she wasn't going to have enough to make ends meet every month, and she'd been surprised at the people who had stepped up. That was why she had been able to go for a whole year without running out of money, and she was grateful to them, but she didn't want to keep asking them to bail her out. Her family and friends would start running as soon as they saw her coming.

Of course, she would do that before she would let any animal starve.

She set the bucket down and reached under her sweatshirt for the belt that she had started wearing.

Her pants had gotten so that they hung on her, and it was cheaper to dig a belt out of her closet than it was to buy a new wardrobe of clothes that would actually fit.

She tightened the belt one last notch—the last notch on the belt.

Her pants gathered together and felt uncomfortable, but she would rather be uncomfortable in her clothes and have more dog food. So she shoved the end of the belt back in the loops and pulled her sweatshirt down.

There. That felt a little better.

As she finished feeding the last of the dogs, she heard a noise before barking erupted, and she looked up, seeing a blue midsize pickup coming down her short drive.

Jones. He often came to help her before he opened his clinic, and the sight of him always made her heart happy. They'd been best friends forever, and he knew of her financial struggles, although he didn't know how desperate her situation was. She'd been getting up earlier so that she could have the animals fed before he came, so he wouldn't see the barrel of food and know that she was almost out. He'd help her. She knew he would. He had before. But she was tired of being a drain on every person who knew her.

Lord, help me know what to do. Should I tell my friends and family how desperate it is? It's close to Christmas, and I know money is tight. I don't want to burden anyone.

Jones pulled in, and she stood, holding the shovel, and waited for him to get out of his truck and walk over to her. He held two steaming cups of coffee, and her heart swelled, grateful that she'd somehow been blessed with such a great friend.

"It's chilly out this morning," Jones said, handing her a mug. It didn't matter which one, since they both took their coffee exactly the same—black.

"You are amazing," she said, lifting her brows and meeting his gaze before she took the mug, blowing a little on the top and taking a hot, burning sip. It warmed her the whole way to her stomach, and she sighed. "Thank you."

"You act like I've never done this before. When I literally do it every single morning."

"I am grateful, every single morning," she said, leaning the shovel against the end of the pole building and wrapping both hands around the mug.

"You should have gloves on," he said, seeing her bare fingers. He laughed and held up a hand. "But, I know, you wouldn't be able to pet the dogs as well if you wore gloves, you couldn't feel them, and they couldn't lick your hand. You'd miss all that stuff, and..." He stopped, and his expression said, *did I miss anything?*

"You're right. Sometimes I wear gloves though," she said, in her defense, although there really wasn't much of a defense. How could she defend herself? It was chilly, her hands were freezing, and the coffee mug felt amazing. She wouldn't need it though, if she were wearing gloves.

Jones rolled his eyes at her.

"Someday a study is going to come out showing that it's actually good for people to touch things, to feel them, to interact with the environment around them, and that gloves stunt people's spiritual and emotional growth and stability."

She wasn't sure such a study would ever be undertaken, but she was fairly certain that it was important, not just for her, but for the dogs, that she pet them every day.

"I'll take your word on it," he said easily, and that was Jones. He just didn't argue. He was one of those people that were sure enough that he was right that he didn't need to convince the rest of the world. He could stand alone if need be. It was one of the things she admired about him. It was part of the reason he'd done what he did when he opened his vet clinic. Instead of doing what everyone else in the world did, and either become a vet at someone else's practice until he earned enough money to open his own or go into debt even more, to make sure he had all the latest and greatest when he opened his practice, he worked hard with what he had.

"Are you done feeding already?" he asked, noticing the shovel and looking inside at all the dogs who scarfed down their food.

"Yeah. I woke up this morning and couldn't get back to sleep, so figured I'd get out and get started."

She had been awake, that was true. But her bed had been so cozy and warm. It should be since she had every blanket in her house on it, because she'd turned the thermostat down as low as it would go without allowing anything to freeze.

It had been forty degrees in her house when she'd gotten up, but she'd gotten warm once she'd gotten out and started working.

"I see," he said, taking a sip of his own coffee and gazing at her thoughtfully before he looked out at the beautiful view.

That was one thing about her kennels; her home was tiny, just a one bedroom with a miniscule kitchen and a small living room, but outside was a million-dollar view.

He took another sip and turned back to her. "That really the reason?"

She stared. He knew she was having financial difficulty, but she was sure he didn't know how bad it was.

He seemed disappointed and glanced down at his coffee before he met her eyes. "I looked in the barrel last night after I left the house. It was almost empty. You would never leave it almost empty going into the weekend, unless...you didn't have money to fill it."

Chapter Two

*J*ones Quebedeau studied his best friend. Her eyes had grown wide, and she looked back and forth.

He couldn't remember in the history of their friendship either one of them ever keeping something from the other. He had to admit, he was a little hurt.

But he understood why she was doing it. She knew that he was taking all of the money he could possibly take to pay off his bills, because he couldn't keep operating his clinic out of a rented garage indefinitely. The owners had just put their house up for sale since their kids were moving them to an assisted living facility, and they intended to unload it as quickly as they could. He was going to have to find a new place for his clinic, and the less he owed on his college tuition, the better off he'd be.

"I'm sorry. I didn't want to worry you. I know you have your own problems."

"I could have given you more hours. I don't have to pay my bills down. It's not like—"

"That's been your plan all along. I wasn't going to ask you to change it because of me. I don't want you to."

He tapped his coffee mug with one finger, wondering if this was the best time to pull out the letter he'd gotten in the mail just yesterday when he got home.

She'd been keeping secrets from him, but that didn't mean he should retaliate, and it certainly didn't mean he wanted to.

But he wanted her to understand that he didn't want her keeping things from him.

That just wasn't the way friendships worked.

"I know that you want me to be able to keep doing what I'm doing, and I do appreciate that. But you realize it hurt me when I figured out that you'd been hiding something this important from me?"

He wasn't sure if she was going to get it, because sometimes a person thought they were doing the right thing, and they just plowed ahead, thinking it was for his own good.

But it wasn't. They were friends, good friends, and good friends didn't keep things from each other.

But he should have known better. Amy knew right away what he was talking about, and she was very good at putting herself in other people's positions.

"I would be steaming mad at you right now if our positions were reversed. I'm sorry."

That was all he needed to hear. He took his free arm, careful not to spill his coffee, and wrapped it around her neck, dragging her head against his armpit, before he ruffled her hair, which was pulled back in a ponytail and didn't have the effect that he wanted it to, and then let her go.

That was as affectionate as they got. But a time like this seemed to call for it.

"I'm going to go to the store as soon as my clinic closes this evening and stock up on dog food, but in the meantime, I wanted to show you the letter that came last night. And before you think I'm keeping anything from you," he said, pulling the letter out of his back pocket and handing his coffee to her so he could open it. "I want you to know that I left my clinic, came here to help you, and then we went down and picked up the kids for the parade and did the parade, and then I brought you home, and it was late when I got the mail. So that's why I didn't tell you about it last night."

"I trust you," she said, looking down at the coffee she held. "I'm sorry. I know you'll tell me everything. I never worried that you might be keeping something from me. And I don't want you to have to worry about that with me."

"I want to give you a hard time," he said, the paper crinkling as he pulled a letter out of the envelope. "But I understand why you're doing it. Truly I do. You don't want me to give up what I've worked for just because things aren't going well for you."

"Maybe God has a miraculous way that He wants to solve this problem. Maybe He's just waiting to drop money in my lap, and I just have to have faith, you know? If I go to you, if I talk to you, you're going to give me money; I know you will. And maybe that's not the way God wants to handle it."

"Maybe not, or maybe it's partially the way He wants to handle it," Jones said without a little bit of irony.

"What are you talking about?" she asked, taking a sip of coffee, and he was pretty sure it was out of his cup.

He held his hand out, and she gave him the other cup back.

It was hers; he could see where her lip balm had made a mark on the rim of the cup.

He didn't care, and she didn't either, and he thought it was odd, because he *would* care with anyone else. But Amy was different. They'd been friends too long to worry about whether or not they got each other's germs. If their germs were going to kill each other, it would have happened a long time ago.

"Let me read this to you," he said. "Actually, let me just tell you what it says, and then you can read it for yourself."

"Would you make up your mind already?" she said, trying to look over his hand at the letter.

"Just be patient," he said. "This isn't something I get to do every day."

"All right," she said cautiously, even though her body still leaned toward the letter.

"So, this is a letter from the lawyer who's handling my aunt's estate. My aunt is estranged from my parents, and I knew her very little growing up."

"I know. You've talked about her a few times. It's Aunt...Edith?"

"That's the one."

"I remember her. Before she and your parents got into that huge fight, you went out to her house for a week every summer. It was the lowest week of the year for me."

"Hey. I quit going by the time I was ten." He bumped his shoulder with hers, and she smiled. Both of them had drunk their coffees to the point where a little bump was not going to spill anything. In fact, he thought hers was almost gone. He should have brought her two cups.

"Anyway, she passed away."

"I'm sorry. I remember you said that. What was it...just before Thanksgiving?"

"Yeah. Sometime in early November. I feel bad that I don't really know, but she never talked to my parents again after they had their big split."

"It's not your fault."

"No, although I could have looked her up when I was an adult. Anyway, I knew she had left me something, and I'd already been contacted by the lawyer. I told him to just send it to me, I didn't need to go listen to a will or anything. But he told me something interesting."

"Okay," she said, sounding a little impatient.

"I've inherited ten million dollars."

"Oh. My. Goodness."

He grunted at her shocked expression. "That's how I felt when I read it. But there's a catch."

"Catch? Is that legal? Can there be catches in wills?"

"I don't know." He was a veterinarian. He had no idea how wills worked. "Basically, I get her entire estate, except for her house and property which she left to her maid, I think."

"What's the catch?" Amy said, and he bit back a smile. He did like to tease her.

"All right. The catch is, in order to inherit the money, I have to be married within one month of her death."

"You have to be married?"

"That's not really that big of a deal. I mean, I guess I kind of thought I would get married eventually at some point. Even though I don't really have any person in mind and never have." Which was true. He and Amy had gotten along so well together, he'd never really noticed the dearth of a girlfriend. He'd had a few dates in high school, nothing to write home about, and he'd met some interesting girls at college, but...he wanted someone who was more like Amy. Someone who worked hard, was unassuming, didn't need to have the biggest and best of everything, wasn't high maintenance, wasn't afraid to give him a hand when he needed it, and didn't get all uncomfortable when he went to help her. And also, who appreciated his help and didn't micromanage him, complaining that he didn't do it right. Also, she was always so grateful for anything he did. Like the coffee he brought, literally, every single morning. She acted like he had brought her an expensive diamond ring or something. He just really appreciated the fact that she didn't take things for granted.

"Well, you probably ought to get your Rolodex out and start digging up phone numbers. Ten million is too much money to just let...what happens to it if you don't get married?"

"Her maid gets it, from what I understand from the lawyer. We had a video call a while ago, but I didn't realize we were talking about this kind of money."

"Well. I... I'm not sure what to say."

"Maybe you should be getting *your* Rolodex out. Because you know that if I need to find a wife, the first thing I'm going to do is get you to help me."

"Yeah. We don't have much time. You should figure out what day she died. If you only have thirty days... She died three weeks ago?"

"Yeah. Probably almost."

"You have a week. One week, Jones. What are you doing here?" she said, her voice raising. "You need to be out...looking for somebody to marry you." She waved with her hands, her empty coffee cup flying as she made shooing motions with her hands.

"I just told you. I'm not going to do it without you. You're going to help me."

"I can't help you! What do I know about the girls you saw at college, and...you never really dated anyone other than Sheena and Brit in high school, and you didn't like either one of them. In fact, if I recall correctly, you spent the next four months after one date with Sheena telling me about how she picked her nose and ate it on your date."

"I'm sorry. If that would have happened to you, it would have marked you as well."

"I wouldn't have gone on a date with Sheena," she said, rolling her eyes. He had to laugh.

"Right." He shook his head, still chuckling but knowing that they weren't getting any closer to solving his dilemma. Ten million. He really didn't want to let that go. And he appreciated his aunt for even thinking of him in the first place. But the marriage clause? It just seemed...tough.

"It's almost Christmas. Just a little over three weeks. How are we going to find someone in the next week who wants to get married two weeks before Christmas to someone that she hasn't dated, ever?"

"Well, that was kind of my problem, but I was hoping, since you're a woman, you could figure it out."

"Since I'm a woman?" Her expression was incredulous. "Are women more capable than men of doing magic tricks?"

"Are you trying to make me feel like I'm so unappealing that no one would help me?"

"Sorry. The problem is most women are not going to marry a guy —any guy, no matter how appealing—they barely know after only knowing him a week. And that's if you take a full week to get to know each other. You won't have a chance to find a second woman to convince her to marry you!" She lifted her hands up and slapped them down at her sides.

"Hey, would you give me that mug before you end up throwing it at me?"

He drained the last of his coffee and then walked back to his pickup, setting them on his hood.

She seemed a little calmer when he turned around, but her movements were still jerky, like she was still agitated. "All right. I need to finish scooping the poop before I can do anything, but I think we need to get started on this right away. It's kind of urgent."

"It's not like I'm going to die if I don't get the money. I mean, it would sure make things a lot nicer, but I'm fumbling along just fine. Although, I did think that it would be really nice to have a brand-new building for my vet clinic, and with ten million bucks, even minus taxes, I'm pretty sure you're not going to have to worry about funding for a really long time. Because an anonymous donor is just going to so happen to give you plenty of working capital every single month."

"That would be awesome if you had that kind of money, but...we need to get it for you first."

He grinned and walked with her to just inside the building where they kept the rest of the shovels. He grabbed one, after sticking his gloves on.

Normally she might tease him about needing gloves to work when she wasn't using them, even maybe giving him a lecture about how feeling things with his skin was important to his mental health, but she was quiet, and he figured she was spinning her brain trying to figure out how to get him the money. He should be more concerned about it, but somehow the idea of getting married left him...apathetic.

They walked to the first pen, with her snapping a lead on the dog to take it out and take it for a walk while he cleaned the pen.

They took turns, with one of them cleaning the pen while the other walked the dog, although they each had their favorite dogs, and they knew who their favorites were, so they didn't have to talk about who was going to walk and who was going to shovel.

Although there were a couple dogs they fought over sometimes. Not today. She was probably too busy thinking.

"You know, my mom knows a lot of people. She has some friends down in Whisker Hollow, and maybe they would know people who know people. I mean, surely they can find a woman who is desperate enough to marry someone she doesn't know, especially if I give you a good recommendation."

"Really? You're going to give me a good recommendation?" He planted the shovel in the ground and tilted his head.

"The very highest," she said as she walked away with a dog.

He went to work shoveling the waste and throwing it in a wheelbarrow that had been left right beside the pen the night before.

Amy, thankfully, believed in doing as much as she could the night before, to make the morning chores easier. A lot of times, he would have to run to the clinic to get there in time to open, and he didn't like to leave before everything was done. And maybe someday he'd be able to sleep in on his days off, but helping his friend meant more to him than staying in bed.

He knew that Amy would get out of bed on her day off for him. She'd stayed up multiple times and gotten very little sleep after going out on farm calls with him.

He owed her.

Whoever he married, that was his requirement: they were going to have to love Amy. Because where he went, she went too.

He finished scooping the poop as she brought the dog back. It wasn't a terribly long walk, but it was the best they could do. Plus, they'd made the pens extra large to give the dogs as much running area as possible. Some of them had been there for a long time.

"Do you have to stay married?" Amy asked as she grabbed a shovel and he snapped the lead on the next dog.

"I'm assuming that we'll stay married forever. That's what marriage is."

"That's what we think marriage is, but if you're getting married in order to get an inheritance, are you required to stay married forever?"

"Just because you're doing it to get something doesn't change the institution of marriage. It's still a lifetime commitment between a man and a woman."

She didn't have a chance to answer him as he walked away. He knew that she agreed, although he could see how some people might think it didn't really matter, if they were just doing it to get something. But to him, if he made vows, he wasn't going to not keep them. Marriage was a holy institution, ordained by God, and one that man had trashed to no end, but Jones wasn't going down that road. To him, marriage was sacred.

Maybe he should just forget about the ten million.

"So you wouldn't even consider an annulment?"

"Don't you have to be Catholic to get an annulment?" he asked as he put Mocha back in her pen and scratched her ears and belly before he walked out and closed the gate behind him.

"I don't think so. I don't know. Still, I think one of the requirements should be that she and I get along, because if you marry someone you barely know, and she decides she hates me, I'm not sure I wouldn't be at your doorstep every day begging you to get a divorce."

"Don't say that word," he said. Not that he was superstitious, but he just didn't want to have anything to do with it. It wasn't a word he was going to talk about.

Maybe someday he'd have to. He couldn't control the person he married, he couldn't keep them from leaving him, couldn't keep them from cheating or whatever it was that led to divorce, he just knew that he didn't want it to be part of his life story.

"You think your mom will have someone in mind?"

"My mom always has answers. She'll know something or someone," Amy said, opening up the latch on the next kennel. She didn't open it very wide, because Molly had a tendency to run off and escape.

He got her hooked and said, "All right. I've got her."

She opened the gate farther. "We can ask my siblings too. They'll know people. Roland probably knows the most, but they might be too young for you."

"Yeah. I don't want someone fresh out of high school who thinks she knows everything, I want someone who's lived a little bit and realizes that maybe there are a few things she has left to learn."

"Is that how we were in high school? We thought we knew everything?" Amy called out behind him as he walked away.

"I know I was. I don't recall you being that way though."

"You're just buttering me up. Because you want my mom."

"I want your mom's Rolodex," he called over his shoulder.

If people heard what they said to each other, they'd probably think they were crazy, but he knew he could say anything with Amy and she'd either laugh or roll her eyes or maybe tell him he was being an idiot, but she wasn't going to get mad at him and never talk to him again. She wasn't going to get mad at him at all, most likely. They'd never really gotten into a huge fight. He could only remember once, and that was over a dog. Of course. Since they were both animal lovers.

They kept working, talking as they did, or working in silence, it didn't really matter. Whatever it was, when he and Amy were together they didn't need to talk in order to be comfortable with each other. It was one of the best things about his relationship with Amy. It was just...comfortable.

He didn't really know if it was comfortable the way it was with siblings or not, since he didn't have any. He was an only child. His mom had mentioned a few times growing up that she wouldn't have minded not having any children at all.

Regardless, he had lived at or below the poverty level his entire life, and he had spent most of his life hanging out with the McBride family and Amy in particular. Mrs. McBride and Mr. McBride had taken him in like he was theirs, and he even called them Mom and Dad.

Neither he nor Amy even thought about his parents as people who could help. They had never been a help. If it hadn't been for the McBrides, he doubted that he would have finished high school, let alone gone on to be a veterinarian.

"What about Lily Wright?" Amy said as she came back from walking Scout, a lab mix, who must have some kind of husky in him, with his blue eyes and curly tail.

"Lily Wright?" he said, aghast that she'd even suggest such a thing. "I don't know what she actually looks like. She wears her makeup so thick it's impossible to tell what shape her actual face is, assuming she has an actual face. I wouldn't want to see her for the first time on our wedding night and be scared. It would be like…sleeping with a stranger." Which was repulsive. He didn't want to be with a stranger. He wanted to be with someone who was going to build a home with him. Who was going to stay with him for life.

"Well, there's Zelly Sanchez," Amy said as they went to the next pen, the occasional barking of the dogs breaking the stillness of the morning as the sun rose higher in the sky, burning off the sleepy haze that had been lying on the tops of the mountains. It wasn't uncommon for fog to roll in, even after the sun came up, obscuring the sun. All one had to do was go down a few hundred feet in elevation to get out of the hazy white. He liked it on those mornings, when the clouds rolled in and made it feel like Amy and he were the only two people in the world.

But that feeling evaporated when she mentioned Zelly Sanchez.

"Amy, really? She's like ultrahigh maintenance. I mean, I stood behind her in the grocery store checkout line once, and she yelled at the clerk for handling her bananas too roughly."

"Well, she's a nice lady."

"Sure, but I'm never going to be able to handle her bananas the correct way." He wasn't sure why he was being so belligerent. Zelly was nice. But she just wasn't...exactly what he wanted.

"What about Opal Huerta?"

Thankfully, he was walking away with the dog, and he didn't have to answer her immediately. Opal wasn't a bad person. But he had to think of something, because the idea of marrying her gave him chills, and not in a good way.

"You know she's a good one!" Amy called as she dumped the wheelbarrow at the refuse pile and turned around to go back in the pen for more.

He walked slowly back, thinking hard until he figured out something he could say. "She doesn't like cats."

He felt a little triumphant as he put Geiser in the pen and unhooked the lead from his collar. He slid back out the door, and Amy shut it.

"How do you know that?" she asked, sounding a little bit exasperated.

"Because she told me so at the clinic. She has a dog, and she was just saying that she was a dog person, not a cat person."

"It doesn't mean she doesn't like cats."

"Why should I take that chance? I bet I'm right, and I can't be married to someone who doesn't love all animals."

There wasn't anything wrong with Opal either, except...she just wasn't Amy.

"Okay, well, all three of those girls are available. And I'm not sure they would marry you in a heartbeat, exactly, but they probably like you enough to consider it." Amy paused. "For ten million dollars."

"Are you saying I'm not exactly a catch?" Jones said as he grabbed a hold of the wheelbarrow and started pushing the load of poop toward the area at the edge of the woods where she spread it out.

"No, I'm not saying that. Actually, I think you have a ton of things in your favor. I mean, you're handsome, you're funny, you are a little bit immature at times, but I think that's just because you're male and not because there's something actually wrong with you."

"Well. Thanks." Maybe?

"I'm just being honest." She paused for a moment, walking beside him with the shovel, so she could spread the poop out. "Yeah, you're even-tempered, you're dependable, a hard worker, you don't shirk your duty, you pay your bills... You're honest, and yeah, I don't think that you should have any trouble getting any one of those girls to fall for you. In fact, I don't know why you haven't been working on this earlier. You know, if you'd taken some time to get a girl and start to cultivate a relationship with her, this wouldn't be nearly so hard."

"How was I supposed to know I was going to inherit ten million dollars from my aunt, only if I was married? Who else in the world has that ever happened to?" And honestly, he wasn't sure that he would have wanted to have "groomed" someone to marry him. He wanted... He wasn't sure what he wanted, but someone like Amy, only...a girlfriend, not a friend. Yeah. That was what he wanted. He just had never felt "it" with anyone else. Not that he hadn't been looking; there were definitely times where he'd long for a wife, but he didn't want to get married to the wrong one and end up regretting it.

"You're supposed to be prepared for any contingency."

"No one in their right mind would have seen this contingency coming. I mean, it's the stuff of dreams. The kinds of dreams that you know aren't going to come true."

"Yeah. I was just giving you a hard time," she said as they reached the edge of the woods and he dumped the wheelbarrow. She took the shovel and started spreading the pile out. "But it would have made it easier, you've got to admit."

"I'm not going to argue with you. But we have to work with what we have. And we have to do it fast."

"Mom will have an answer," Amy said with confidence. He hoped she was right.

Chapter Three

"I'm sorry, I have no idea of who in the world you can get to marry you within a week," Marjorie McBride said as Amy and Jones sat at the bar in front of her.

It was Friday morning, early, and her three grandchildren, the children of her oldest son Gilbert, had not awoken yet. Once they did, her day would be full, taking care of them, feeding them, making sure they had things to play with that weren't going to hurt them and would keep them from getting into trouble, and in between all that, praying for Gilbert and Sally, his wife.

"But, Mom, you know everyone," Amy said, picking up a cookie from the plate that Marjorie had set in front of them. If there was one thing that she had learned as a mom who was alone with her six children a lot, it was that cookies solved a lot of problems.

She joked about it, though she really did try to depend on the Lord to fix things, but... This seemed like it was way too big for even prayer.

Therefore, cookies.

"She's right, Mom. Surely you know someone?" Jones said,

looking at the cookie Amy held and snapping it out of her hand. "That one's not cooked. You hate them like that. It's mine."

Jones ignored the fact that Amy had already taken a bite out of it, and consumed three quarters of the cookie in one mouthful.

"That's because I'm focusing too hard on trying to get you a wife."

She almost laughed at the two of them. They were like brother and sister only... She didn't think they quite felt about each other the same way Amy felt about her other siblings. And she was pretty sure that Jones didn't feel the same way about Amy as he felt about her sisters.

They would say that that was because they were such good friends, but Marjorie had a tendency to think maybe that wasn't entirely true.

"These are really good, Mom." Jones's brow wrinkled. "Did you tweak your recipe?"

"I did. With the kids here, I'm baking more than what I usually do," she said easily, tilting her head. "What do you think?"

It didn't surprise her at all that Jones was the one who noticed. Amy had a tendency to put her head down and pull blindly forward. Jones was the one that kind of came along behind, looking at things and noticing stuff.

"These are new?" Amy said, without giving her a chance to answer.

"I think they're amazing. Although, I don't think I've ever eaten a cookie of yours that I didn't like in my life. Well, except for those fruitcake cookies that you tried back when we were, what, fourteen or so?"

"Oh goodness. The notorious fruitcake cookies." She was never going to live them down. Even Jones gave her a hard time about it. "You make a woman not want to try anything new by your constant harping on her failures," she said in a lightly scolding tone. One Jones knew to be joking. If she were scolding him, he would know it.

"Mom. Fruitcake cookies. What in the world about those two words would make you want to try it?" Amy could be a little outspoken, although it was part of what made her endearing. One always knew where she stood. Except for her financial issues. Marjorie had a feeling that part of her need for Jones to get the ten million dollars was because she was hoping she would have a new benefactor for her sanctuary.

Marjorie loved that Amy loved animals, but she wished that Amy didn't love them quite so much, and could have a real job, and not worry her mother so much, especially about how in the world she was going to survive.

"It sounded new and interesting. Plus, the idea of a fruitcake is kind of a good one, it just...doesn't always go together very well," she said, wrinkling her nose. She always wondered why fruitcake had such a bad rap. She didn't really like it herself, and she didn't know too many people who did, but what she had just said—the idea had potential. The reality just didn't live up to it.

"Can we focus?" Amy said, taking the cookie that Jones handed to her. It was dark and crispy, the way she liked them. He reached around the plate for one that was more his style, doughy in the middle.

They were opposites in a lot of ways, but there was so much about them that fit together perfectly. Even their oppositeness worked out. If she almost burned a pan of cookies, Amy would eat them, and inevitably there was always a pan or two she took out too early, and Jones loved those.

That was the way they were in life. Amy was the one who had all the ideas and blew into town with guns blazing, while Jones provided her backup, cleaning up the mess and helping her turn her dreams into reality. She often thought about how good they would be together, but neither one of them ever seemed to notice that the other one was right there, available, and perfect.

Lord? Is this Your way of pushing them together?

So many of her prayers as a mother were silent. Her kids would flip out if they knew the things she prayed about them.

She hesitated to suggest that they think about each other as a potential solution to their problem, as they both munched thoughtfully on cookies, and she turned around to get the batter ready to make pancakes for the kids when they got up.

She had forty-five minutes before she had to get them on the bus, but in her experience, forty-five minutes went by in a flash when a person was trying to herd three small children.

"You guys are here early," Roland said as he walked out from down the hall, pulling a sweatshirt down over the top of his T-shirt as he did so, carrying his boots in his hand.

She preferred that her kids not wear shoes in the house, but they had too many kids for everyone to leave their shoes by the door. Otherwise, there would be a mountain to cross as soon as a person stepped into their house. So instead, everyone just took their shoes off and carried them to their rooms.

It had taken years for her to train her children to do that, and then, once they were trained, they moved out.

It was a pity that children stayed in a person's house until they were old enough to really be a blessing, and then they left.

That wasn't entirely true. By the time her children were eleven or twelve, they were doing as much as she was around the house.

Still, she missed them after they left. But she had grandchildren instead, and they helped remind her that she was glad that she wasn't raising young children anymore. She was older than she used to be and got tired a lot faster.

Maybe if she had a husband to help her. But Sam had died, and while he had been a good man, not perfect, but he tried, she wouldn't mind finding someone to share the rest of her life with. But the logistics of that... She had six children. How were they going to blend their families? What about grandchildren? Were they both responsible for everyone's grandchildren, or did they each have their own? That didn't really seem like a very good marriage, when one person had their own grandkids, and the other person had their own grandkids, and neither one of them shared grandkids.

It just seemed messy and complicated and full of potential to have hurt feelings.

She wasn't sure she wanted companionship bad enough to try to navigate that minefield.

Plus, she was old and rather set in her ways, if fifty-five was considered old.

It was old to her twenty-year-old self, but once she hit her mid-forties, seventy felt young.

"Mom, you need to think. Please?" Amy asked, sounding like she was talking with her mouth full.

"I'm thinking, honey. But what you're asking is rather impossible, unless you find someone that Jones already knows and likes. A friend. A friend who would be willing to build a relationship into more." She paused and turned around, a cup of flour in her hand, and put the other hand on her hip while tilting her head. "Do you know anyone like that?"

Jones got it before Amy did. She could see it coming over his face like the sun coming up from behind the mountain.

It wasn't quite as glorious, but it still made Marjorie bite back a smile. The guy looked absolutely gobsmacked, like the idea of marrying Amy had never, ever occurred to him, not once in his life before.

Marjorie wanted to roll her eyes while she turned around, but she refrained. Being a mother did nothing if not teach her self-control.

"Jones just doesn't really have a lot of girls that are friends other than me. I mean, Isadora is getting divorced. I suppose she knows him well enough. I'm pretty sure that Terry and Judd are going to be a thing here. But..." She turned to Jones. "Terry could be a good idea? You and she have grown up together."

"I think your mom might have been talking about you," Jones said, and Marjorie had already turned back around. This was a moment she didn't want to miss.

She held the bowl against her stomach as she stirred, not too much, because if she stirred pancake batter too much, they got flat instead of puffy.

"Me?" Amy said, and for a moment, Marjorie thought she was going to fall off her barstool. "Mom, tell him you weren't talking about me," she called out, sounding like she meant it, then she ended in a softer voice, "Were you?"

"Can you think of anyone better?"

"Sure. I can think of four billion people who are better. I'm always barging into things and sticking my foot in my mouth and jumping into stuff without thinking about it, and besides, Jones and I are just friends."

"And sometimes friends make the best marriage partners," Marjorie said, wondering when her voice had gotten that wise old tone that said sage in the woods dishing out wisdom for tokens.

"Jones?" Amy said. "Aren't you going to say something?"

Jones lifted his brow, and then, smart man that he was, he grabbed two cookies and shoved them both in his mouth.

Roland came over and grabbed a cookie, his boots clomping on the floor as he shoved the cookie in his mouth and pushed his hands into his coat sleeves. "I don't know what you guys are fussing about. You're perfect for each other. Everybody thought you were going to get married ten years ago. Just do it already." He took the cookie out of his mouth and waved at Marjorie. "Have a good day with the urchins, Mom."

Grabbing his hat from the hook by the door, he shoved it down on his head and walked out.

There was total silence in the house after he left.

Chapter Four

my could not believe that her mother had suggested such a crazy idea. The idea that she and Jones would get married? That was ludicrous, although there was a part of her that had to admit that there was a certain rationalism there that she couldn't deny.

After all, she and Jones *could* get married. They practically lived together anyway. They didn't sleep at each other's houses, but they did everything else together. Always. Other than his job, which half the time she was there with him anyway.

And he was always helping her. Her parents were his parents, which... That's what made everything weird. She had never thought of him like a brother, but that's kind of the way he was. But there was something there that she couldn't quite put her finger on. She'd never quite acted like he was her brother. She didn't quite feel the same way about Jones that she felt about her brothers.

Honestly, she would have said that she liked Jones more. But that was actually kind of playing into her mother's hand, and almost agreeing with her, when Amy knew that she absolutely could not agree to this. Unless Jones thought it was a good idea. And then, at that point, she supposed they could talk, but until then, it was her job to fight this. Jones was too easygoing, and her family could kind of ramrod things through, especially if they thought they were right. She ought to know, she was the poster child for that.

No one had said anything since Roland had left, when Robert came running into the kitchen.

"I'm up!"

"Are you ready for breakfast?" her mother asked as he came running around the dining room, doing a lap around the table before ending up in the kitchen in front of his gram.

"I'm starving!"

Roland always got the kids up before he went to work. And from what Amy had seen, Robert woke up running. The other two kids weren't quite that bad, but Robert didn't seem to ever stop.

She wasn't quite sure how the teachers got him to sit still in school. He wasn't a bad kid, he was very obedient, but he was constantly moving.

"I'm ready to put them on the griddle. Are you dressed?"

"I was too hungry to get dressed!" Robert said, sounding like he was begging for food.

"It'll take you exactly three minutes to put your school clothes on. Now go do it, and then we'll sit down."

When she had been growing up, they had been homeschooled. Typically their mom did a Bible lesson while they ate, and after they got to Robert's age, one of them had always been assigned to make breakfast, so she didn't often see her mom in the kitchen cooking breakfast.

And she had never been told that she had to change her clothes first. She could stay in her jammies all day if she wanted to when they homeschooled.

No adults had said anything when all three kids tramped out, hearing the pancakes were about to go on the griddle.

"I'm back!" Robert said, running again, holding something green and leafy in his hand.

"What's this? What's this?" he asked, running into the kitchen and stopping at the counter in front of the griddle, holding up the piece of greenery he had found.

"Oh goodness. That must have fallen off the doorpost," her mom said, looking over at the doorway where the hall met the living room. "You just put it on the counter, and I will put it up later."

"But what is it?" Robert insisted.

"That's called mistletoe."

"Mistletoe?" Marissa said, looking curiously at the piece of greenery in Robert's hand.

"Isn't that the stuff if you stand underneath it, people are supposed to kiss or something?" Lucas said. He was the oldest and possibly the one who was most aware of the fact that his mom was dying. He wanted to help with everything, and Judd had been taking him under his wing, taking him along to help with any odd jobs that he picked up, including blowing leaves out of their own yard. He even paid Lucas for it, and there was a bit of maturity about Lucas just in the week since he'd started hanging out with Judd.

It was crazy what adult interest could do for a child.

"That's what's supposed to happen," Marjorie said. "But it's usually only around Christmastime, and it's mostly for decoration."

"It's how our town got the name, Mistletoe Meadows."

"Let's see if it works!" Robert yelled, running around and climbing up on the back of Amy's and Jones's stools, holding the mistletoe over their heads.

"Now you have to kiss!" he said, waving the mistletoe around.

"Get down before you fall," Amy said, laughing but feeling awkward with Jones for the first time in her entire life. Even her mom suggesting that they maybe should get married hadn't made her feel as awkward as Robert saying that they needed to kiss.

But rather than obeying, Robert started talking louder. "It's not working! You need to kiss. That's what this is supposed to do. It means to kiss!"

"Yes! You have to kiss. It's the rules!" Marissa said.

"Gram, tell them they have to do it. That's what the mistletoe is. It means that you have to kiss," Lucas said, looking to his gram to solve the problem.

Amy wanted to tell him that she was a little bit too old for her mother to be telling her who she should and shouldn't kiss, although she didn't want to say that. She didn't want Lucas to think that she wasn't going to obey her mom if her mom told her to do something. Of course she would. Her mom wouldn't command her to do something ridiculous, and Amy believed that no matter how old a person was, they should honor their parents. A lot of times, that meant doing what they wanted you to, even when you didn't want to or were old enough to not.

But she didn't have a chance to say anything, because all three kids were talking over each other, arguing about the mistletoe, and whether it worked or not, whether or not their gram should step in. The noise was almost deafening.

"Maybe we'd better do this, just to keep your mom from losing her mind," Jones said, leaning close and whispering low, loud enough that he could be heard over the voices but not so loud that if she disagreed, he would look like a traitor.

She jerked her chin, and then she called out, "Fine. Watch closely, guys, because we're only going to do this once." Then, she gave Jones a look that said she was sorry for her family, a look she'd given him a million times in the past. Anytime they did anything terrible, she was always the one who had to apologize, but when they did something good, Jones pretended like he was one of them.

It wasn't fair. But they'd had a good time laughing about it over the years.

The kitchen quieted down, and she leaned forward, intending to give Jones a quick peck on the lips. But she didn't want to hammer him with her nose, so she slowed down just in time, and their lips touched softly, almost sweetly.

It wasn't the kiss she had intended. Not at all, she thought as she slowly moved her head away, wondering if Jones felt the same shocking...was that the right word? Shocking feelings that she did. They were very unexpected.

Chapter Five

_J_ones was thankful the children were in the kitchen. They cheered after the kiss and then started asking for breakfast, and their gram started giving them directions on setting the table and getting things ready as she got three more pancakes off the griddle and set them down in front of them.

He hadn't eaten so many cookies that he wouldn't have been hungry, but the kiss had stolen his appetite. He had not thought about kissing Amy before, and even now, he'd figured she was just going to brush his cheek or something, but he should have known better. She always went into things headfirst, although maybe she'd just been going too fast to get where she was aiming.

He let out a humorless laugh. It was so Amy. They'd also satisfied the kids, and he should be just fine with it. But instead, he was left reeling. Feeling like his world had shifted, and things would never be the same. But that might have been partly because of the ten million dollars and the fact that Roland and Mom had both suggested that Amy be the girl he looked at.

At first, he rebelled, the same way Amy had, only she always reacted more vocally than he did.

But, wow. Now... Did that change anything?

He thanked Marjorie for pancakes, waited for the kids to be served, and they all were quiet again. Normally Amy and he would both be up helping Marjorie, but he hadn't even given it a thought. He'd been so engrossed in trying to figure out what to do, and then the kids feeling like a whirlwind, and then the kiss.

"I ate too many cookies," he said low, while the kids and Marjorie talked at the table.

"Me too," Amy said softly beside him.

"But I don't want to hurt your mom's feelings."

"Me, either. I'll have to throw up later."

"I was going to hang out with you today, but I just changed my mind."

She laughed, as he figured she would. It didn't matter what he said, she always thought his jokes were funny. Even if they were corny and dumb and she'd heard them a million times. She always acted like it was the first time.

So they both sat there, forcing the pancakes into their mouth, eating as quickly as they could without even talking about it.

Still, the kids were done and on their feet, and Marjorie was working on making sure they had their backpacks and other things together, before he and Amy finished and gathered up the plates, putting them in the dishwasher.

Amy grabbed a rag and wiped the table and counter, and he rinsed off the bowls and utensils that Marjorie had used to make pancakes, sticking those in the dishwasher and starting it.

He felt as at home in the McBrides' kitchen as he did in his own. More so, since it was actually a kitchen and not just a refrigerator and stove with a short counter between them which is what he had over the garage of the place that he rented.

It served him just fine, on the few, very few, times that he ate by himself.

"Ready?" Amy asked as she came over and rinsed the rag off in the sink.

"Yeah."

"You guys have a great day at school," Marjorie said as she kissed the head of each child as they walked out the door to wait for the school bus.

"I want to check my mail," Amy said as they walked out the door.

Jones figured she was probably going to check her mail to see if there was a check in it. He hoped there was, for her sake, but it brought back the thought that maybe marrying her wasn't such a bad idea. She could use that ten million dollars far more than he could. Of course, she made her choices. She decided to open the pet sanctuary almost directly out of high school, since she was already taking in stray dogs and cats. She could have gone to college, or she could have started her own business or even gotten a real, regular job.

But she'd chosen to go get donors for her pet sanctuary and devoted her life to her animals. She was just reaping what she sowed and doing what she wanted.

He knew he should be hands off, but she was his friend and he... loved her. Because he loved his friends.

Friends.

Right?

He thought again about that kiss. It was just a simple kiss. Something he could have given any woman and not felt bad about it. Although he didn't typically go around kissing people on the lips.

Actually as he thought about it, he wouldn't mind doing it again. Just to see if it was as...shocking? Something. Just to see if he felt the same way after the second kiss.

He wasn't going to suggest that to Amy though. She didn't need to have any idea that he was thinking about kissing her. Again.

They left, telling Marjorie that if they didn't see her before, they'd see her Sunday at lunch. He and Amy rode in the horse-drawn wagon to pick up the kids with Judd driving. So it took them a little longer to get there after church, since they had to drive the kids home. Still, all the family had been really good about it, and they never started eating without them.

They got in his pickup, and as he was pulling out of the drive, which was just about three minutes from where Amy had her pet sanctuary, he said, "Sorry about that."

He wasn't even sure what he was apologizing for, he just felt like he had to say something. Amy meant more to him than anyone else in the world, and he didn't want to ruin whatever he had with her. Even though his entire life seemed to be spiraling, maybe not out of control, but fast enough that he felt like he needed to grab something to hold onto, and the only one that ever felt sturdy enough for him to clutch was Amy.

"Oh goodness, don't worry about it. We did it to shut the kids up. And to make it so that Mom didn't lose all of her hair this morning. Just most of it. I don't know how she does it every morning."

"How is Sally doing?" he asked, figuring that Amy probably didn't know anything more than what he did. It was just something he asked in order to change the subject. He'd apologized, she'd accepted it, and they could move on from it for now. She wasn't upset. It was Amy. If she were upset, he would know.

"The same. Worse. I don't know. Treatments aren't working, they want to send her home and call in hospice, but Gilbert doesn't want her here, with him solely responsible for taking care of her. He's afraid she's going to die. That's what Mom said. And I was just sitting there thinking, but she *is* going to die."

"That's the point of hospice. To get to die at home. Surrounded by people who love you, and in surroundings that are familiar."

"Yeah. Although, Mom's house is hardly familiar to Sally. They've been there, but it's not like her house."

"Is Gilbert going to move back once..."

He didn't want to say "once she died," but that was what he meant.

Amy didn't make him say it. She understood. "I don't know. I can't say, 'hey, what ya gonna do after your wife kicks the bucket,' you know?"

"Yeah. Some people can accept those kinds of things, but Gilbert seems like he wants to keep fighting."

"I would appreciate that, if I were Sally. But I think everyone has admitted that if she's going to get out of this, only God can do it. She might as well come here to Mom's house and get hospice, because God can do a miracle here just as well as He can in the hospital."

"Yeah." He wasn't sure what he would do. Of course he didn't have a wife, but Amy was the closest thing... But no. He wasn't going to marry Amy.

"You mind stopping at the mailbox?" she asked, even as he had turned his turn signal on and pulled into it, opening up the little door and pulling out some letters.

He was going to tease her with them, but he just handed them over. The top one looked like a bill, and he figured she probably wasn't in the mood to get teased about that.

The silence felt loud as he shut the door, put his window up, and waited for a car to go by before he crossed the road and pulled into her drive.

"Bills, bills, bills... Hey! I think this is a check!" Amy said as she pulled the envelope open.

"Careful. You're gonna rip the check," he said as he stopped the pickup beside her tiny little car. He didn't figure the size should fool anyone, because he'd seen Amy haul at least four dogs around in it, and not small ones.

"It is! I can buy dog food! This is awesome." She bowed her head and said quickly, "Thank you, Lord," and then raised her head just as fast and turned her shining eyes on him. "He sent me a check. He doesn't want me to close down yet."

He couldn't help but smile. She was so over-the-top exuberant. Of course, she'd mellowed from when she was a kid. Robert, whose only speed was a run and whose only voice was ten thousand decibels, reminded him a lot of Amy. Of course, there were some boy-girl differences, but Amy always ran on full speed, and while she didn't yell at the top of her voice every time she wanted to say something, she could get excited and forget to modulate her tone.

He smiled affectionately at her as she waved it around and did a little dance on her seat before yanking at the door handle.

"Is that okay? Do you mind if we go get dog food?" They always spent his day off and the weekends together. But usually they chatted about what they wanted to do, laid out the needs that they had, whether it was grocery shopping for the week or visiting the kids they would be picking up on Sunday morning for the wagon ride to church.

Somehow, they managed to get it all done, and somehow, they managed to do it all together, and even more amazing, now that he thought about it, was they managed to do it without getting tired of each other.

"Sure thing. All I need to do is pick up a few groceries for lunch this week, but nothing else."

"Did you decorate your apartment?" she asked, like he hadn't spent nearly every waking second with her and might have somehow found time to do it when she wasn't around.

"It's too small. And there's no point. I got that little tree up in the office, and that's going to do it for this year."

"That's what I got done," she said as they walked side by side to the front door of her house.

She opened it, and he held it while she walked in. She didn't bother to lock it, and he'd stopped asking her to. When she first moved out of her parents' house so she could be closer to her animals to make it easier to take care of them, he tried to get her to lock it, and she resisted. Saying that it was Mistletoe Meadows, and not only that, but she had fifteen dogs on the place. No one was going to be sneaking in.

Speaking of dogs, her three small house dogs, all rescues, jumped up and came bounding over to greet them, wagging their tails and begging to be petted.

Amy knelt down immediately, and he knelt down beside her. He wouldn't have become a vet if he hadn't loved animals to begin with, but Amy might have taken it just a bit far.

Still, he didn't have any pets, so she more than made up for it. When he went home, it was a little bit quiet in his apartment above the garage where his office was, but sometimes he appreciated the escape. Not from Amy. From the animals.

"Hey, Chatty. What's the matter?" Amy said as her most vocal dog, Chatty, whined and scrambled to keep her attention.

Casper, older and slower than the other ones, was content to allow Jones to pet him. Dragon, aptly named, showed his teeth to Chatty, who immediately hunkered down and rolled over, showing her belly.

"Guys, you gotta get along," Amy said, the same thing she said a hundred times to them every day.

Amy stood and walked to the counter. Her house was tiny, almost as small as his apartment. The living room was just a touch bigger, and she had been able to fit a queen-size bed in her bedroom. He ought to know, because he'd helped her put it there.

"Let me get this deposited, and I think they'll give me enough of it in my account right away for me to get at least a couple of bags of dog food." She spoke as she grabbed a pen and signed the back of the check.

As she reached over the counter for the pen, his eyes caught on her waist as her sweatshirt came up.

"Where'd you find those jeans? They look like they're about six sizes too big." He noted the way her belt pulled the waist tight. There were big gaps where the material gaped.

And then, as he looked a little closer, he realized that she'd lost weight. That was why the material was gaping and the jeans looked so big. She'd been wearing bulky sweatshirts, not necessarily to hide it, but because it was cold out.

"These things? I've had them forever," she said offhandedly as she used her phone to take a picture of the front of the check.

Yeah. And even this summer, they hadn't been so big on her that she'd even needed a belt.

But of course, she lost the sponsorship from the Richmond Rebels, and when that happened, the townspeople had jumped in to help her out, but he supposed that most of those were one-time donations, and people needed to be reminded that she was here.

"When was the last time you did a sponsorship drive?" he asked, thinking that maybe she was in more dire straits than what he thought.

"I don't know. I know I need to, but I hated to do it around the holidays. People are so tight with money already, and prices are up. It's killing everyday families, and I hate to hurt them even more."

She had been cheering about being able to buy dog food, but she hadn't said a word about getting herself groceries. He quit scratching Dragon's head as he stood and wandered into her kitchen.

It was neat if not tidy, and there wasn't a whole lot of stuff sitting around.

Typically he didn't snoop in her cupboards. If they were cooking, he wouldn't hesitate to get in and get whatever he needed, but it felt just a touch odd for him to open them without needing anything. But he knew exactly where she kept her dry goods, and he cracked the cupboard door.

Some rice, three cans of beans, and two boxes of pasta. He thought there might be two cans of chopped tomatoes, but he couldn't see the label and didn't touch them.

He heard the check flip over, and figured she was probably taking a picture of the back, as he moved to the refrigerator and opened it.

There were half a dozen eggs inside, and that was it. Not even milk. There was some butter, a jar of ketchup, and mayonnaise.

She'd basically been eating beans and rice. Maybe pasta, although he wasn't quite sure what she was going to put on the pasta. Chopped tomatoes?

"All right. Yeah, it's saying that part of the check is available immediately. That's awesome. I'll be able to get enough to last the weekend, and I can go back on Monday and get more." She broke off abruptly. "What are you doing?"

He hadn't realized he was staring at the refrigerator, running through the implications in his mind.

He shut the door and turned slowly to face her. "Your pants are baggy because you've been losing weight. You've been losing weight because you're starving yourself because you don't have enough money to feed yourself and the animals." He wanted to say, *why haven't you told me?* But he had to ask himself, why hadn't he opened his eyes and looked at her? Why had it taken him so long to figure it out? It wasn't like they didn't work together all day every day.

He knew it was a baggy sweatshirt, a fact he didn't really pay attention to. He should have. Should have paid a lot more attention to her than what he did.

"I never look at you," he said softly. Almost to himself.

"You just realized I'm beautiful. Is that what you mean?" she asked, shoving her phone in her pocket and lifting her brows, asking him if he was ready to go without saying anything. And also saying, *what's going on? Why are you being so weird?*

"I just take advantage of you. You're just...here."

"I take advantage of you, too." She lifted her shoulder like it wasn't a big deal. "That's what friends do. They rarely appreciate each other until something happens, then when they need someone to lean on, your friend is standing right there, shoulder near, tissue at the ready, just there waiting for you to tell them what you need, so they can go do it. That's what friends do."

"You're starving," he said.

"Don't be ridiculous. This is America. People don't starve in America."

"You ate pancakes at your mom's house, and cookies." He'd eaten just as much as she had, and he wished he wouldn't have brought that up, because the kiss had ruined his appetite and hers as well.

She should have gotten as many pancakes down as she could,

and come to think of it, more than once she had grabbed something and been eating it as she walked out of her mom's house.

But they didn't eat at her mom's house a lot. Enough to keep her from dying of starvation apparently.

"So, what are you trying to say?"

There might have been something similar to irritation in her tone, but she was never truly irritated at him.

"Never mind. Let's go," he said, nodding at the door and starting to walk. It was just two steps until he passed her, and he was tempted to reach out an arm and wrap it around her waist, gauging for himself how much weight she'd lost, except he never touched her that way, so he really wouldn't be able to tell how different she felt.

"You don't have to get all snippy about it," she said as she ripped the check up and threw the pieces in the garbage as they walked out the door.

"I just feel like you're not telling me everything. Like you've been hiding something big from me, and I should have known. You should have told me."

"There wasn't anything to tell you. And I don't want to talk about this. Your car or mine?" she asked as he shut the door behind them, and they walked down through the yard.

"Mine," he said immediately. She probably couldn't even afford gas. "Maybe this is something I think we should think about."

"What?" she asked as they got in the pickup together.

"My inheritance. The ten million dollars. The clause that I have to marry. Everyone you suggested gave me the shudders, every time I thought about spending the rest of my life with them. You and I spend all day every day together, and I haven't gotten tired of you yet. And you still put up with me, somehow. So... Maybe your mom and Roland were not crazy after all."

"You can't be serious. You and me get married? That's..."

He almost expected her to end that comment with, "gross," or "disgusting," or "unthinkable," but she didn't. "It's what?"

"I just never thought about it like that before. You're…Jones. That's who you are."

"I already kind of feel like your family is my family, but I never think of you as my sister," he said, and he felt hesitant about saying that, since he was admitting it and they hadn't really talked about it before,

"I don't think of you like my brother, except… You're better." She fell silent after that, and they didn't say much on the trip to town. He tried not to go too often, because it was a long drive, and typically they just went on the weekend. Sometimes after he got off work in the evening and she was done with the dogs and they didn't have anything else to do, they'd take a trip, and then they'd go hiking or something on the weekend.

Neither one of them ever had an issue with what the other one wanted to do. It was like they were so into each other that they just floated along together.

Although, he knew that wasn't true. They were so opposite that neither one of them had much in common.

"You think the reason that you and I get along so well is because we trust each other?"

"Maybe. What do you mean by that?" she asked, slanting a gaze across the seat from him, and he wished he would have asked instead what she was thinking about.

Although that was a question he never asked, so it would be very telling. He wanted to know what she thought about the kiss.

And maybe about getting married to him.

"I just mean that sometimes when you're with someone who likes to do things that you don't, you resist. You don't really want to do what they want to do because…you feel like if you give in, you're just constantly going to be giving in and you're never going to get your way? You know what I mean?"

"Yeah, I guess I kinda see that. You mean trust as in, you can do what I want, because you know that in the very near future, I'm going to be doing what you want, and it's just something we do."

She lifted her shoulder, tilting her head a bit as she looked out the windshield. "I never really thought about it as a trust thing, but I think you're right. I do know that I can hold my nose and do some things with you, because you'll hold your nose and do some things with me."

"Not everything that I do with you is me holding my nose and just doing it."

"No. I didn't mean that," she said, laughing a little bit.

They might not especially want to do things sometimes, but it never felt like one of them was holding their nose. They had a good time together, no matter what.

They were quiet as they rolled down off the mountain and passed through the little town of Whisker Hollow. There was a nice grocery store just off Main Street, with the feed store beside it, and he pulled into the parking lot.

"Usually I don't have to tell you to talk to me, Amy, but you've been awfully quiet."

"You've been quiet too," she said, grabbing the latch and yanking.

He got out as well.

"You have your grocery list?" she asked, as though she had just thought about it.

"I do. We can get the dog food first."

"It will fare better sitting in the car," she said, and they strolled to the feed store, getting the bags she needed and taking it back to the car before they got his groceries.

He noted she didn't get anything, and he'd wondered how he had managed to not notice that she hadn't been buying much.

"I guess I assumed you were just eating more at your mom's, with Gilbert, and everything that was going on with him, and your sister Isadora as well."

"Yeah. There's been a lot of turmoil at Mom's house, and all the grandkids always running around," she said.

"So, I'm not super hungry, but I've been hearing so much about these breast cupcakes. What do you say we go try them out?"

"Nora's cupcakes in any shape are delicious."

"You've had Nora's cupcakes with me, and we both agreed that they were delicious. But we haven't had these cupcakes."

"I don't know, this is a little bit embarrassing."

"I heard it was an accident."

"I heard that too. I also heard that she ended up dating Leo Lipinski of the Icebreaker hockey team. Which is...pretty big."

"Yeah, girls say a hockey player is better than a veterinarian any day," he said, wondering why he was annoyed. He didn't typically get upset or annoyed about anything Amy said, although she didn't typically talk about other men. Was that really what bothered him? That she was talking about another guy and he was jealous?

"Sorry. I just meant he was famous. You know, girls typically swarm to guys that are famous or have done big things, and I don't know. It's just a girl thing."

"It could be a guy thing to do. Like with a supermodel."

"True," she said, nodding her head and then looking up at him with narrowed eyes. "Are you saying I'm not a supermodel?"

"You're skinny enough to be a supermodel right now. But you lack the height."

"And the gorgeous facial features, great hair, and a deep-seated desire to walk naked or mostly naked down the runway. Yeah. This kid was not destined to be a supermodel."

"I wouldn't be able to hang out with you all day most days if you were a supermodel. So for one, I'm thankful, for two, who said you weren't gorgeous?"

He knew that was crossing the bounds of their friendship, a line they never even came close to. Maybe it was all the talk of marriage, but he couldn't let her get away with saying that.

"I say it. I mean, I can tell you all the reasons why I'm not a cover model, if you really need me to. But it has to do with my cheekbones here and—"

"Amy. I don't care where your cheekbones are. Well, we are talking about your facial cheeks, right?"

Her mouth dropped open. "Where's Jones? What have you done with my friend?"

He grinned. "I think it's all this talk about marriage."

"Really? I would have mentioned the M word years ago if I'd realized it was going to get you to call me gorgeous and start talking about my cheeks. Actually, no. That was a little awkward."

"What?" he asked, realizing that he didn't feel nearly as awkward as he thought he might. It was Amy. He could talk to her about anything. Even cheeks, upper and lower.

"Okay. I admit it. This conversation is not nearly as awkward as I would have said it would have been, if yesterday someone would have asked me. But... I don't know. You're just easy to talk to."

"I feel the same way about you," he said, pushing the cart to the side of his truck, where he grabbed the few groceries he had bought and stuck them behind the seat while Amy took the cart and put it in the cart return.

"Cupcakes?" he asked when she came back.

"If you say so. Although, I feel like you're just trying to put weight on me now."

"No. I really want to see these cupcakes. I've heard so much about them, but just from clients."

"You should have said something about wanting to go down and grab some. I'd have been on board for that."

"Talking about breast cupcakes with you just seemed weird, but... It wasn't. We got through it just fine."

"Just like we got through that kiss just—" Amy's mouth snapped closed, and her eyes shot to his, wide and horrified.

She slapped a hand over her mouth.

"Oh. We're not talking about that?" he asked, his brows going up, humor dancing in his eyes.

"I wasn't going to. I mean, we did it, and it's over."

"Is it?" he asked, not really expecting her to answer, just knowing that for him, it wasn't.

Chapter Six

_It_ turned out Nora's cupcake shop didn't have the breast cupcakes that they were famous for. Everything was Christmas.

The owner, Nora, was such a sweetheart, and Amy enjoyed going in every chance she got.

They walked back toward the truck, not sitting in the shop to eat since they had groceries in the car, with Amy licking the icing off her cupcake first, the way she always did when she ate one.

Jones ate the cake part first and saved the icing for last.

She said she put the kiss behind her, but she really hadn't. She wanted to. She wanted to stop thinking about it, but the more she tried, the harder it was. Especially when she thought about what it would mean when Jones got married.

"So if you find a girl who will marry you, you know you and I probably won't be doing stuff like this anymore?" She spoke the thought foremost on her mind.

"Sure we will. We'll just have my wife with us." He spoke lightly, and she knew he was joking. No wife was going to want to tag along with a man and his best friend when that best friend was a woman.

"I think you know enough about women to know that that would not be possible," she said.

"I do. I'm kidding. I guess I never really thought about it before. It wasn't an issue. And now... I don't know, I guess I'm giving more credence to what your mom and Roland said. But not if you're not interested. After all, who really needs ten million dollars anyway? Right?"

She laughed and bumped his arm with hers. He took a step sideways and then corrected himself and bumped her back.

"We have the whole weekend. We don't have to make a decision right now. I mean, we don't even have to talk about it right now. You're not going to get married to anyone else before Monday."

"Sure. And if someone else pops up before then, we'll just roll with it. And if no one else does..."

"So that makes me feel like I'm the last resort, and it doesn't feel very good," she said, and she wasn't really joking. Even though she tried to keep her tone light. It was true. Like if he couldn't find anyone else, he'd go to her, although she knew that wasn't what he was saying at all.

"You're my first choice. Honestly. I told you what I think about those other girls, I can't stand the idea of them just...hanging around. You know? Like, I could spend a day with them, or maybe an afternoon, but I think I'd be happy when they left. With you, I never want you to leave. I know because... I'm not some sappy, lovesick man who can't function by himself. It's just because I enjoy your company."

"Do you think that might be what people fall into after the really hot phase of their relationship burns out?" she asked, and she should have known he would have no idea what she was talking about.

"Say what?" he asked.

"I don't know. I just heard people say that you know, you have strong feelings when you're in love, and then you get married or whatever, and they just fade away and you're left with a good friendship. You're still attracted to each other, and intimate too, but just... Those crazy feelings don't last forever."

"Yeah. I suppose I can see how that's true. So you think we act like an old married couple?"

"I don't know. Maybe?" She wasn't sure what she was saying, but she had to admit that she was warming to the idea.

"My phone just buzzed, hang on," he said, balancing the very top of the cake part of his cupcake with all of the icing on it as he dug for his phone.

They were almost at the pickup, and they stopped right at the front of it, with her finishing off the cake part of her cupcake and him checking the number.

"I think this is forwarded from the office," he said before swiping with his pinky finger, trying not to drop his icing.

"Jones Quebedeau," he answered.

Amy didn't try to listen. Jones would tell her everything after he was done. Instead, she put her hand out, with her brows lifted, offering to hold his icing for him. He stopped mid sentence, his eyes getting big, his mouth opening, and he mouthed, "no!" as he turned and put his back to her, protecting his icing.

He was right. She probably would have licked it.

She looked around the parking lot, pulling her jacket a little tighter as she saw folks hurrying to and from the store, stocking up on baking goods to make Christmas cookies and pies as the decorations of Whisker Hollow fluttered on the lightpole at the side of the parking lot. The sky was overcast gray, like it often was in November, and the temps weren't terrible. They warmed up to almost sixty.

Still, jacket weather. At least for a Southerner like her.

Although it was warmer down here than it was on top of the mountain. It almost always was.

"I'll be right there," Jones said as he turned, using his pinky to swipe up again and holding out his icing to her so she could take a bite.

"Are you sure?" she asked, her eyes reminding him that he had just yanked it away from her.

"I thought you were offering to hold it. You and I both know exactly what would have happened if that had been the case. I would have had nothing."

"You don't even like the icing," she said.

He grinned sheepishly, acknowledging her words, before wagging the icing and the top part of the cupcake that he held in his hand. "You want some?"

"Wow. I even get the first bite," she said as she took a bite, and he laughed.

He was able to shove the rest of the icing in his mouth, and they stood there eating before he swallowed and could speak.

"How do you feel about putting a uterus back in?" he asked, licking his fingers, before looking her in the eye.

"I feel good about it," she said. Then she laughed. "It could be ninety degrees out, or it could be snowing. So, since it's about sixty, which is not terrible, I say, yeah. Let's go put a uterus in."

He laughed. "I figured that's what you'd say. I told him I was here and I'd be right there. It's Otto Lee, who lives about ten minutes outside of town here. It's actually fortuitous that we're here. If you don't mind, we need to hurry. He said the cow was alive, but if we don't get that thing back in, she won't be for long."

"Yeah."

He didn't get a whole lot of farm calls, but she'd done twisted stomachs with him, a couple twisted uteruses, and she'd put several uteruses back in with him, too.

"Do you have everything you need in your truck?"

"Yeah. I've got my bag with me, so we should be good."

He always threw that in. Wherever they went. He didn't always get called, but sometimes he had a pet emergency, and he never knew what he might have to do. They'd found it best to be prepared.

"I'm sorry about your groceries," she said.

"I bet Mrs. Lee will put those in their fridge for me, until we're done."

She realized he was right as they pulled out of town, heading up the mountain toward the Lee farm.

"I don't think I've ever actually been back here," she said as he turned down a dirt road and ran over cattle guards. They served in lieu of a gate to keep the cows in.

"What do you think about after we're done here, we'll go see Gilbert and Sally?" he said as the barn came into view.

"I think that'd be really nice," she said, meaning it. She wished she knew what else she could do for her brother. She helped her mom with his kids as much as she could, but losing his spouse was just such a hard thing, and unfortunately, when it was a spouse, a person felt something that no one else in the world understood other than those who had gone through it, and no one else in the world could really help them with. It was when a person had to lean on God the most.

"He said they were in the side pasture, the one before the house. This must be it."

He started to turn left and stopped in front of the gate while she hopped out to open it.

She held it while he drove through and closed it behind him before getting back in.

"She should be up at the top of the hill. He was going to make sure I got some hot water and some towels."

"I remember the last time we did this, my arms felt like rubber by the time we were done."

"Mr. Lee should help us. We're not doing it by ourselves."

"I know. I couldn't believe that guy just stood there and watched us."

"He didn't know any better, and the little bit that he did do made me feel like we were better off without him helping."

"Yeah, true." The fella didn't seem to know how to handle cows, and if she recalled correctly, he was a suit from DC who drove out to his "cattle ranch" and played farmer on the weekend. Not that he couldn't learn how to farm, because anyone could. But he couldn't learn if he wasn't willing to get his hands dirty.

"There she is," she murmured, seeing a big black cow lying on her side as they crested the hill.

"He said he had the calf in the barn. It wasn't up yet, but he felt like it was going to make it."

"I see. That's what he was doing?"

"Yeah. He called me as soon as he saw the cow and said he'd be back up once he got the calf into the barn, although if he could get it up and feed it, he was going to do that."

"Did he have colostrum?" She'd been helping him long enough to know that newborn calves needed that for immunity.

"Said he did." He didn't need to say anything more. Sometimes guys said things that weren't true, just to appease the vet.

She didn't really understand that. They were only hurting themselves. It wasn't like Jones was going to get the army down to make them do what they were supposed to do.

Most farmers did try to do the best they could for their cows. Money was often an inhibiting factor, but their cows were their livelihood, so of course they were gonna take care of them as best they could.

"All right," Jones said as they parked beside the cow. "It's obvious this is the cow, she's down and her uterus is right there. She still breathing?"

"Looks like it," she said. "I see her side moving."

"All right. I need to get a few things together, and then we'll hope that Mr. Lee gets back here with that water, and maybe he'll even take our groceries to the house."

Amy looked down at the house. It was probably a quarter of a mile away, maybe almost half. "Do you want me to walk them down?"

"Nah. I'd rather have your help here. This is a tough job for one person."

"I'm not sure one person could do it," she said, remembering the last time, but if he didn't have her, he'd do his best.

It turned out that they were able to get the uterus back in, although it was just as much of a struggle as Amy remembered.

By the time they had it taken care of, it was lunchtime, and her stomach was growling. The pancakes and cupcake had worn off for sure, although she didn't have a whole lot to look forward to in her cupboard.

"I appreciate you coming out on such short notice. My regular vet was at a wedding and suggested you."

"I'll do in a pinch, but it's not really my thing. I think your cow should be okay. If she gets up in the next half an hour or so, I'd give her a pretty good shot."

"I appreciate it. She's a good cow, and I'd hate to lose her."

Jones nodded, and Amy figured Mr. Lee would have said that about any cow.

She had already carried his things back to the truck and brought his invoice booklet out.

Since he did such few farm calls, it didn't make sense for him to pay a service to do invoicing online. He just did it by hand.

He took the invoice from her and nodded his thanks as Mr. Lee continued to tell Jones about the calf and how it had eaten and seemed to be fine.

Jones offered to go down and check it out, but Mr. Lee told him that if the mom made it, he was going to see if he could get the calf back on her.

Amy wasn't sure that was a good idea, but Jones didn't say no, and they shook hands while Amy put the booklet away and came back to stand beside them.

"Call me if you need me. I'm heading over to the hospital later, but I'll be around for another hour or so."

"All right. I'll let you know," Mr. Lee said, nodding his thanks again, as he got back in his truck and headed for the gate.

Amy and Jones got in their truck and followed him through.

Amy didn't have to get out since Mr. Lee was waiting to close the fence.

"Thanks a lot. I appreciate your help."

"Sure. Not a problem. I enjoyed it, and I always learn something new. Sometimes I think it's easier to work with cows than it is dogs and cats. At least you don't have to worry about getting bitten."

"Just kicked," he said, shuddering, and she remembered that he had gotten hit in the thigh once when the cow had been thrashing.

"Is your leg okay?" she asked, looking at the muddy spot on his jeans where her hoof had come up and hit him.

"I'm going to live."

"That's a relief. I suppose if you die, you're not going to get the ten million. And that means I won't get it, because I'm the beneficiary in your will, right?"

"If you marry me, you will be," he said, like an offhand comment, except...they didn't have that kind of relationship, and it ended up being one of those comments that came out in the air and just hung there, filling up the cab of the truck with its reverberations.

"Sorry. I shouldn't have said that. I...guess I'm thinking about marriage a little bit too much."

"No. You're right. That's exactly correct. I just...don't know what to say."

"We said we were going to talk about it. And think about it. Since we're thinking about it, if marriage comments come out, it's probably normal, right?"

"Absolutely. You're the one who has ten million dollars hanging on it."

"You kind of do too," he said, looking over at her and lifting a brow.

She knew he was right. She did have ten million dollars hanging on it. "But I don't think about it like that. I think about it more like..."

She wasn't sure what to say.

Neither one of them said anything, and he drove to her house, where he had some extra clothes. He took a shower while she threw his groceries in her refrigerator and then boiled some pasta and tried to throw a few spices in the tomatoes so it tasted like spaghetti sauce. She wasn't sure she succeeded, but he came out, his hair wet, his T-shirt clinging to his shoulders like she hadn't noticed before, and ate the pasta without comment.

Jones actually was handsome, she thought as she threw a covert glance at him. He wasn't ruggedly athletic, and he did have a tendency to be a bit of a nerd, but she loved that. She really wasn't into ruggedly handsome guys. Never had been. Or the athletic type. They were fine for some girls, she supposed, but when she had been talking about Leo Lipinski, the hockey player, she hadn't meant anything by it. Other than that was something that attracted a lot of girls. Just not her. She loved the fact that Jones would stop what he was doing to help her on his day off and was willing to drive to some farmer's field and save a cow's life.

She had to admit she was kind of proud of him. In fact, it made her awfully proud of him. There weren't a whole lot of guys who could do that. And of the guys who could, there were even less who would.

"What in the world are you looking at?" he asked, looking down at his shirt. "Did I drop tomato sauce all over me or something?"

"No. I was just thinking about how nice it is to be friends with someone who cares."

"Who cares?" he asked, stretching out his brows and wrinkling his nose like he thought she was nuts.

It was an expression he used often.

"Yeah. You didn't have to go to the farm today. You didn't have to take care of that cow. You decided to do it because you care. And I love that about you."

"Who else is going to do it?"

"That guy's regular vet. I mean, yeah, he was going to a wedding, but you were going to visit someone in the hospital, someone you may never see again. I just mean that you stopped what you were doing and you helped. I know you do that no matter what."

"Well, if the wedding is mine, I'm probably not going to go and help with a cow."

"If I'm the one that's with you at the altar, we're going to go do it."

They laughed together as she realized that she'd gone from being awkward talking about it to being able to joke with him. That was a good first step.

Chapter Seven

"This wasn't too bad," Jones said as he finished up the spaghetti. It definitely wasn't spaghetti sauce, but it wasn't terrible.

"Thanks. Not too bad. So in other words, you don't think you're going to need to have your stomach pumped in the next three hours." Amy rolled her eyes, and he laughed.

She got up from the table and went back to take a shower while he cleaned up the dishes. They didn't even talk about it. He had gotten his shower first while she cooked, so it just made sense that he cleaned up while she got hers.

He thought about that for a while. He supposed if he did find some random stranger up the street to marry him, eventually they would have that type of relationship. Where they just did things without talking about them. Where they were opposite, but that could turn into their biggest strength, the way he and Amy were. But why would he try to get that with a stranger when he already had it with Amy?

That just made sense. He would be just as happy with Amy as he would be with someone else, wouldn't he? After all, he was already friends with her. It wouldn't be that hard to be more.

He thought about that kiss again. Thought about the mistletoe that Robert just happened to pick up that morning. Of all mornings.

Lord, was that You trying to show me something? Am I really that dense?

He didn't have to answer that question. He knew he was dense. While he did believe that God cared about man and guided the events of their lives, he also believed that God gave them opportunities to have their free choice. Where He gave them principles to see, and they could make decisions within those principles, where anything was correct.

In marriage, for example, as long as the person that he was thinking about was also a Christian and lived for the Lord, agreeing to have the kind of marriage that God wanted, he could choose anyone that fit those criteria. The principles that God laid out.

That was what he believed anyway. He knew that there were other people who believed that God had a perfect person, a soulmate, just waiting for them to find, and that if they made one wrong choice, they could miss their opportunity with that person forever.

He just didn't think that things had to be that exact. Mostly because he figured that God knew that humans were never going to do things that perfectly.

Amy didn't have a dishwasher, so he did the dishes by hand and put the little bit of spaghetti that was left over away. While he did so, he saw his groceries in the refrigerator and made a mental note to grab them and drop them off at his house on their way to the hospital.

Amy came out not that long afterward, wearing a white blouse with a vest along with her jeans and boots.

He looked up from the refrigerator, forgetting that he had the door hanging wide open while he looked at her.

She'd put a little bit of makeup on. He'd seen her wearing it before; typically on Sundays, she wore some, and if they were going somewhere other than shopping or with her family.

He wasn't quite sure why women did that, although he did like the way she looked with it on. Maybe not better than with it off though. He just liked the natural Amy. Knowing that there wasn't anything hidden. He didn't have to worry about whether or not he was going to be scared of the way she actually looked on their wedding night when she took her mask off. The way he honestly was with a couple of the girls that she'd suggested.

"What?" she asked as she stood in the doorway, waiting for him to say something.

"I don't know. You just look...good."

"Try not to sound so surprised. It's bad for my ego."

"You don't have an ego," he said, rolling his eyes and closing the refrigerator door, turning away from it. "Don't let me forget to take my groceries."

"I'm ready to go if you are."

"Did you call and tell them that we were coming?"

"I can text Gilbert on the way. I'm pretty sure visiting hours are over at seven, so it's not like we have to worry about whether or not we're going to get in."

"Two people at a time?"

"That's what it was last time I was there."

She had gone once while he was at the clinic during the day.

She petted Dragon's head and then squatted down and gave Casper a few scratches as well.

Casper was the one who usually hung out with him, and interestingly, he'd never thought about Amy possibly being jealous. It was almost like Casper was his dog. And that's just the way it was.

Maybe that was when it really hit him, hard, that if he were to get married to someone else, he wouldn't be hanging out in Amy's house all the time. On his days off, his wife would most assuredly expect him to, if not be with her, at least be at his own house, not with some other woman.

"I wish this would never change," he said.

She looked up, her brows drawn down. "What? Are you talking about the dogs dying?" She glanced at Casper. He was the oldest.

He bent over and scratched his ears, and then he said, "No. Just this. Life is good, you know?"

"Yeah. I've been thinking about that with Gilbert. He's got a big change in his life. And I know he never dreamed this would happen. But how do you pick up the pieces and go on from that?"

That hadn't been what Jones was talking about at all, but she was right. He never knew when something like that would happen. He tried to imagine losing Amy. What would life be like without her? He did everything with her, other than what he did at the clinic, and half the time, she was there. She filled in for his receptionist when she took off, and she worked as a vet tech when his tech needed a day off. She cleaned it with him and talked with him about what he'd like to do if he actually ever did get to expand.

If he got married, he could expand immediately.

"That's kinda a serious subject for this time of year." Amy sighed. "We're supposed to be thinking about Christmas and the joys of the season."

"Speaking of the joys of the season, I heard we're supposed to get a storm next week."

"Really? That must be new."

"There were some rumblings about it yesterday, but this morning on the way over, I was listening to the radio and they were saying that it looked like things were coming together, and we might get up to a foot."

"Really?" she said, straightening up and wiping her eyes. "That's a lot."

"I know. But they always go wild and crazy, and then they ratchet it down, until it finally comes, and you get a dusting. Everybody ends up disappointed."

She laughed, because she knew as well as he did that that was true. The weather people were fearmongers.

She walked to the refrigerator and grabbed his groceries, and lifted her brows at him.

She didn't have to ask him twice, and he went to the door and opened it for her. And then he opened the passenger side pickup door so she could put the groceries in the back before she got in.

"Thanks," she said, hopping in the seat and looking a little surprised when he closed the door for her.

He didn't usually stand and do that. But he'd been thinking. It was funny how a couple little sentences could change someone's entire life. How a letter, a letter with information that had the potential to upend everything he had been doing and planning on, could change his world.

"It was nice of my aunt to choose to pass away during the holidays," he said, knowing that he could say that to Amy and she wouldn't take it the wrong way. She'd know that he wasn't happy that his aunt died.

"It was a great Christmas gift, wasn't it?" she said, laughing.

"Well, the idea was a great gift, but the more I think about it, the more I think I'm just going to let it go."

"What? Are you serious? You'd give up the money?"

He lifted a shoulder and didn't say anything.

"Jones?" she said, a little bit of the warning in her voice.

He gave her a grin and then turned his signal on to turn into his place.

He looked at the sign out along the road, Mistletoe Meadows Veterinary Clinic, and thought about how he and Amy had put it up.

They had bags of quikrete and had gotten the holes dug, and then it started to rain. He thought that it was going to be a disaster, but somehow they got the quikrete mixed up and put in the holes, and so far, the sign hadn't blown down. That was five years ago.

He'd been fresh out of school, and she'd been ecstatic to have him back full-time. That was why he had put his hours to four days a week. He took emergencies sometimes in the morning and sometimes in the evening, and he was on call all weekend. But those hours allowed him to spend time with his best friend, whom he'd missed dearly in college.

Even now, he couldn't believe he'd spent so much time away from her. Although they talked every day, messaged a lot, and FaceTimed almost every evening after she was done feeding her dogs. She'd even helped him study.

He got out, and she hopped out on her side, grabbing the bags and arriving at his door as he got it open.

She knew where his refrigerator was. He didn't have to follow her in, and he didn't, just waited at the door while she threw the stuff in the refrigerator and came back out.

"You are seriously thinking about giving up the money?" she said as she walked in front of him and stopped.

"Well, I could rush into a marriage that might not last a lifetime, but I'm doing just fine without the money. I'd love to pay off my student loans, and I'd love to support your pet sanctuary more, but otherwise, I don't need millions of dollars. I'm happy the way I am."

"I'm happy the way I am too, but the money would be nice. For you. You could build a vet clinic, you could have everything paid off, you could not work if you chose not to or take cases for free."

She lifted her shoulders, and he shook his head. "I can't believe you, of all people, are trying to convince me that I should do something crazy, like marry someone I barely know, and at this point, I don't even have a name in mind, and just so I can get money. I mean, is a lifetime of misery with the wrong woman worth ten million dollars?"

She huffed out a breath, looking him in the eye, but he knew she was thinking about it and she had basically agreed with him.

Her lips flattened, and she looked away before she walked out the door.

He followed her out, but he knew his argument was valid. He was right. He might not have a good marriage, and it just wasn't worth it.

They were backing out when she said, "You know, you and I have talked about this with my family at times. And I believe that you could have a good marriage with anyone as long as you have the same values and morals. As long as you agree on the basic things, religion being the most important. After all, you don't want to be married to someone who isn't going to go to church with you or isn't going to spend eternity in heaven with you."

"I agree. I think you can get along with anyone, and I think that's why God doesn't tell us or have more specific requirements beyond the command to be not unequally yoked with unbelievers. That's the main requirement. Now of course, you want someone who will keep their vows and will follow the biblical roles for husband and wife, but if they're a Christian, they should."

"You have to be careful of those people who say that they're Christians and really aren't."

He nodded. That was true. He knew several unhappy marriages where one of the spouses had been deceived before they were married by a spouse who pretended to be a Christian but was just going through the motions because they wanted to get married to that particular person.

He felt like that was the greatest deceit of all. Especially when the person who was doing the deceiving knew that the one that they were courting wanted a Christian spouse. And wanted to have a Christian marriage. He didn't understand why they would pretend to be different.

That was not his problem in this instance though. So he let the idea go.

"So... What you're saying really doesn't hold water," she ended finally.

He laughed. "I guess. But..." He couldn't finish. He didn't know. He just couldn't get on board with any of the girls that she'd suggested. Sheena, Brit, and Lily and all the others they'd talked about were all really nice girls, but how could he tell her that none of them were her?

"So what's the problem?" she asked, and then she added, "I promise, I'm not asking you because I'm trying to push you into doing something you don't want to do. And I'm definitely not asking because I'm hoping to get a cut of that ten million. I assume if you get a wife, she's going to have ideas of her own as to how she could spend the money, and I'm guessing that if you married the right woman, or maybe in this case the wrong woman, ten million dollars could disappear pretty fast."

"I agree with you completely. I don't think it would take any time at all to spend it, if you have the idea that it was just all there for you to blow."

He didn't say anything else about that, but changed the subject and started talking about the storm some more and how much he loved snow. Amy hated it. Mostly because it made her job harder, while all he had to do was go downstairs to open his clinic, although if it snowed a foot, he'd definitely be closing. He was a Southerner to his core, and Southerners didn't drive in the snow with any amount of skill. And he preferred to keep his truck undented. Not because he drove into someone but because of his patients' parents sliding into his truck.

They pulled into the hospital around three o'clock. It seemed busy for a Friday, but what did he know about hospitals and how busy they typically were?

He didn't spend any more time than he had to at hospitals. Ever.

But Gilbert was like a brother to him, and he *was* Amy's brother, and if they could come visit him and be a little bit of support to him, he felt it was the least he could do.

They parked and slowly got out of the vehicle.

Neither one of them really wanted to go into the hospital. And the mood between them had become sober.

There was no more talk of marriage, no joking about it, and no thoughts of ten million dollars. It was about Gilbert and the fact that he was slowly losing his wife.

And the pain he must be feeling.

"When I texted him, he said they were in the same room," Amy said softly as they walked in the doors and nodded at the people standing at the counter, ready to offer help for anyone who needed it.

"All right. That was on the second floor?" he said as they walked toward the elevators.

"That's right. Number 237."

Both of their voices were softer, and Jones had to resist the urge to run away. He didn't know what he would do if he were losing Amy.

Amy wasn't his wife.

But she could be.

He heard that voice, and a day ago, he would have thought that that was crazy, but now... He couldn't imagine the pain if God were to take Amy from him. Although, he knew God promised to walk with him through anything, so apparently he'd be able to handle it if He did.

They were silent as the elevator doors closed, and both of them stared at the closed doors as the light moved to the number two, and the doors opened.

He waited while Amy walked out first, and then he put a hand on the small of her back for just an instant as he walked up behind her. Just a touch to reassure her that he was still there, or maybe it was to reassure himself that they were together.

Whatever it was, she looked up, not in shock, but in gratitude, as though she had needed that human touch, that little bit of reassurance.

He smiled down at her, and she returned the smile, both of them sad, feeling heavy.

They stopped at the nurses' station, told them who they were looking for, and the nurses waved them on, sending them back.

The door was open, and Jones could see Gilbert sitting in the chair beside Sally's bed, his arms on his knees, his hands clasped together, his head down.

He could be sleeping, but Jones guessed he was probably praying.

"Hey," Amy called, her voice subdued, as she tapped on the door, and then they walked in.

Gilbert's head lifted, and his bloodshot eyes and ragged face brightened a bit as he watched them walk in.

"Hey there. You guys got in okay," Gilbert said, starting to rise.

Jones put a hand out. "You don't have to get up," he said, coming in and glancing at Sally, who lay in the bed, tubes attached everywhere, her eyes closed, her face deathly pale.

Gilbert swallowed, glanced at his wife, then jerked his head.

"Good to see you. It's quiet in here." He took a breath, as though he were forcing himself to be a part of the living. "How are the kids? Did you guys see them today?"

"I can tell you a story about them if you want me to," Amy said from beside him, and he knew immediately she was going to tell the mistletoe story.

He cringed inside, because he wasn't sure that she wanted to be reminded that they'd kissed earlier today. Was that really just today?

And how was she going to tell that story?

She glanced at him, and he could see questions in her eyes. He knew she was wondering if it was okay that she share the contents of the letter.

He nodded, and before Amy could say anything, Gilbert laughed. "You guys are so funny when you do that."

"Do what?" Jones asked.

"What you just did."

"What did we just do?" Jones said.

"Just looked at each other, had a whole conversation without speaking a word, and you understood everything you said, and you made a decision. It's like the rest of us don't exist." Gilbert shook his head. "You know, I always wished I had that with my wife, and we never really did." He ran a hand through his hair. It looked like he'd been doing that a good bit, the way it stuck up all over the place. "Not that there's anything wrong with that, but you guys just have some kind of special bond."

"Funny you should say that, because that has a little bit to do with what your kids did this morning."

"Okay, now. Tell me they didn't do anything terrible? Did Mom decide to kick them out?" He grinned a little as he said that, because he knew his mom wasn't going to kick anyone out, and they knew it too.

Jones snorted. "Your mom would pay you to move in with her. She loves those kids. And they didn't do anything wrong today. It was just a little bit funny."

"All right," he said, sitting back with another glance at his wife and then indicating the two chairs on the other side against the wall. "You guys can sit if you want to. She's unconscious. She's been that way since yesterday. I...I'm feeling that she's probably not going to wake up. I keep asking the nurses, and they don't really say anything, and of course the doctor just says that's what's going to happen. The cancer's gonna take over."

Gilbert closed his mouth and lifted his shoulders, hunching a bit, while Amy and Jones sat down. Jones allowed her to pick her seat, and she chose the one closest to Gilbert. Then, after she sat down, she got up and scooted even closer so that she was almost touching the end of the bed.

He scooted his chair over too and said, "I guess if a nurse comes in, we'll probably have to move."

"I should have brought her home. Hospice would have been better. Then you guys wouldn't have to drive so far to see me, and I'd see the kids, but... I didn't want them to see their mother like this."

"We can bring them here if you want us to," Amy said.

"You think that's what I should do?" Gilbert asked. "Because Sally said when we came here last time, she kissed her kids and hugged them, and they all were happy, and she said, 'I don't want them to come in and see me dying. I want this to be their last memory of me.'"

He looked out the window before turning back to the bed. "I want to give her what she asked for, but at the same time, she's leaving me, and I'm going to have to raise my kids myself for the rest of my life. Are they going to be mad at me because I didn't tell them that their mother was dying? Are they gonna be angry because they didn't get one last moment with her, even though she's not talking and they can't communicate with her?" He ran a hand through his hair again and sighed. "I don't know what the right choice is. They're so young."

"I don't know either. You just have to do your best," Amy said, and Jones nodded.

"When they get older, we can tell them that you struggled with what to do. I think that they'll just have to understand that sometimes there's no roadmap. You weren't prepared for this type of thing and are just doing your best."

"Yeah. I felt like my place was beside my wife, and she was afraid to die at home. She thought she might...suffer." He took a breath. "And I didn't want to be responsible for deciding whether to call an ambulance or whether to resuscitate her, or see her struggling and... I don't know. What do you do in that instance?"

Jones had never thought of anything like that. He hadn't considered it at all. But it was a good point. He didn't want to be home with someone who was supposed to be dying, who...was suffering, then what would he do? Call an ambulance? Take them to the hospital? They'd made the decision to die at home.

"I didn't want my kids to see that. I mean, it might mark them to not feel like they got to say goodbye to their mom, but how would it mark them if they saw her at home, struggling, or in pain, or unable to breathe, or... I didn't know it was going to be like this." He nodded at his wife, unconscious in the bed. "Maybe if I had, it would have been different. Or maybe it wouldn't have been like this if we'd been home."

"I don't know. I guess every person is different, and you can't tell until you're going through it," Amy suggested.

"I just... I want to do the best thing for them. And it's funny, when you have children, you have a spouse to talk everything over with. Every decision, you can discuss what's best, get a different viewpoint, and go from there. But now, I don't. I have to do this on my own, and I wasn't expecting that."

He fell silent, like he had more to say, but he was forcing himself to go quiet, because what good was railing at God for taking away the one person he had to talk to about the decisions they would make for their children together?

Since God was the one. He was in charge of everything, and He got to decide whether Sally lived or died.

Jones glanced at Amy and thought about the time that they'd had together. Maybe he'd taken it for granted. He hadn't thought about anyone dying this young. Sally wasn't any older than either one of them. The cancer had been unexpected, and her death the same. It could happen to anyone, anyone at all.

It was a good reminder to cherish every day.

And that's when he realized, there really wasn't anyone else in the world that he wanted to spend his days off with. There wasn't anyone else in the world that he wanted to spend his evenings with. There wasn't a single person in the entire world that he had fun with like he had fun with Amy. That he could talk to like he could talk to Amy. That he enjoyed being around like he enjoyed being around Amy.

Whether he got the money, or whether he didn't, it just seemed to make sense to marry her. But women didn't want things to make sense. They wanted romance and flowers and hearts and stuff he didn't know anything about and would feel awkward even attempting with Amy.

"So tell me about the kids? What did they do?"

"Well, Robert came out holding mistletoe, and he asked Mom what it was."

"Oh goodness." Gilbert laughed. It was a sad laugh, but still, he was smiling. Jones was glad Amy had decided to tell the story.

"Of course, Mom was busy trying to make breakfast, and we told him it was mistletoe. The purpose of which was when a couple stood underneath it, they had to kiss the person they were with."

"Oh, great. The things you guys are teaching my son when I'm not there."

"Well, our town does have mistletoe in its name, so he ought to know what it is."

"And?" Gilbert said.

"So anyway, the other kids came out. They were hungry. It was before school, and there were a lot of things going on, and before we knew it, Robert was standing behind us, one foot on my stool, one foot on Jones's stool where we sat at the counter, and he held the mistletoe above our heads and told us we had to kiss."

"Oh. Robert's a brave one."

"What's that supposed to mean?" Jones said, confused. He was expecting Gilbert to laugh.

"That's what everyone thinks about you two, but Robert's the only one who apparently has the guts to say it. I'll have to congratulate him when I get home. Was he able to get you guys to kiss?"

"We weren't going to, but we felt bad for Mom, so Jones leaned over and said we ought to do it just so we could shut them up. It was complete chaos in the kitchen."

"I see," Gilbert said, lifting a brow.

"So, we made sure they were all watching, and then I gave her a quick peck on the lips to satisfy your son."

"You know, we should grab that mistletoe and throw it away. What do you think of that?" Amy said, looking at him with her head tilted. Almost as though she were trying to change the subject so that Gilbert couldn't say anything more about how everyone had thought that that was what was going to happen between them.

"Maybe because you want to do it again," Gilbert said, grinning, looking between the two of them. "Everyone in the family will say we all had bets placed at one point or another as to when you guys were going to get together. Personally, I thought you were going to be married before Jones went away to college. I didn't think Amy could survive without you for eight years. And I thought at some point, you'd come home and decide that being a vet wasn't what you wanted."

"Are you serious?" Jones said, having trouble believing that. "People were betting on us?"

"Sure. I had a bet with Roland for fifty bucks. I had to pay up, because he said you guys wouldn't get married until you came home for Christmas."

"Wow. Have we ever acted like boyfriend-girlfriend?" Amy asked, looking at Jones.

"You guys don't have to act like boyfriend-girlfriend. You act like a very old couple. You blew right by the girlfriend-boyfriend stage and just landed in the old married couple stage."

"That's no fun," Jones said, giving Amy a look which she didn't have too much trouble interpreting. He was pretty sure she understood that he was just going to go along with the flow, because it was getting Gilbert distracted from what was going on with his wife.

"Old married couple?" Amy said, shaking her head. "What an insult."

"It's not an insult. It just means you guys are so comfortable with each other, and you have a subtle language of your own. That's... really nice. Sometimes I'm not even sure I knew my wife." His voice trailed off, and he looked at her, lying still and silent in the bed. "I guess I just always thought that there would be tomorrow, you know? I figured we had our lifetime to get to know each other and do all the things we wanted to do, and now I realize that wasn't true."

"I guess there's a lot of lessons to be learned there. I was actually thinking the same thing as I was sitting here. That we think we have a lot of time, and we take it for granted. People, mostly. We just think they're always going to be there, and we don't realize that they might not. So we need to take the time to do what we can today, while we still have time."

Jones knew his words were serious, and Amy looked at him, nodding, like she understood perfectly what he was saying.

"So tell me, should I bring the kids in?" Gilbert looked helplessly at Jones, who didn't have a clue of what to say.

"Do what you think is right. And don't second-guess yourself. If you want to honor Sally's last request, do it. And then tell the kids that's why you did. And they'll just have to accept it. And if you want to bring them in, because you think it's necessary, do that. Just... Do the best that you can, because no one can do anything more than that," Amy said, her voice confident, but low and quiet.

"All right then. I'm gonna stop guessing about it. I know my place is here beside her, but the kids are staying home. I'll just tell them that she's gone, when she goes, and I'll deal with the fallout if I have to. After all, I suppose they could be just as mad at me for bringing them in and ruining what could have been their last memory of their mom, which was somewhat happy."

She hadn't been in the best shape when she'd gone to the hospital, but she'd at least been upright and smiling. Now, she was so still and white that she almost looked like she was dead already.

"Are the doctors giving you any hope at all?" Amy asked after a bit.

"None. They look for signs of death, and apparently they saw it on her feet today. I don't even know what they're looking for, but they said it wouldn't be long." Gilbert looked down and pursed his lips. "I guess, I guess at this point if it's going to happen, I just wish it would. I'm tired of thinking about it. Not that I want to wish her leaving any faster than what I have to, it's just... If she's not going to get better, I need to get home to my kids."

Those were harsh words, and Jones flinched a bit. He kind of understood what Gilbert was saying though. To him, Sally was already gone. She wasn't talking, she wasn't moving, and while it seemed like he was holding out hope that a miracle might happen, it most likely wasn't going to and he just wanted to be able to get home.

Maybe that wasn't the most compassionate thing that had ever happened, but Jones kind of understood. And no one who saw Gilbert would doubt that he was being torn apart by his wife's death.

"I'm sorry. Maybe I shouldn't have said that. But it's hard for me to wish that she'd hang on the way she is. Like, if she's going, all right. Go."

"We understood exactly what you were saying. And it makes sense. No one can blame you for it. I don't think anyone could give you a hard time for the way you've been at her side the entire time and still try to do as much as you could with your kids too. You've got to be exhausted."

"Yeah," he said, sighing.

They sat for a while, occasionally saying something, but mostly just being there with him, until darkness started to settle in and Jones stirred. All the time that he'd been sitting there, Sally hadn't moved at all. Her breathing was low and slow, and the machines beeped beside her, but there had been no sign of life.

"Would you like someone to stay with you?" Jones asked. Gilbert startled when he spoke.

"No. I'm not afraid to be alone. Actually, God's here, and that's just as good as anything. But she never said what she wanted. Maybe she'd like to have the whole family. I don't know."

A nurse came in just then, and Amy and Jones stood up, moving their chairs for her to be able to get around. She walked slowly, moved carefully, and spoke softly.

"I think, I'm pretty sure anyway, if you'd like to call the family in, this would be the time. I'm guessing that she's going to go sometime this evening or tonight."

"All right. Thanks," Gilbert said, his voice cracking a bit, but his eyes remained dry. Although, they were bloodshot and his face was haggard like he hadn't slept in a week.

It wasn't long until they walked out of the hospital, quiet and sober. Was there any other way one could be after spending the afternoon like that? But he wouldn't trade it for the world.

"Thank you so much for doing that. I know it had to have been miserable for you. But I just felt like Gilbert needed people to be beside him."

"He didn't sound like he wanted to call anyone to come in."

"Maybe he just wants to spend the last few minutes with his wife alone. He...is right. I never really thought that they were a great couple, you know? Like I can't really put my finger on it—"

"I know exactly what you're talking about. They were okay, they got along just fine, but it felt like they were missing a deep connection that a lot of couples have. Although, I think they would have stayed married for life."

"Oh, I know they would have. Both of them were totally devoted to each other, but I think sometimes they wished that they would have chosen differently. Like they weren't best friends."

Jones said, "Yes. Exactly."

They had just exited the elevator and were walking toward the doors when Jones's phone rang.

"It's your brother," he said as he looked at his phone before swiping it.

Amy's eyes got big, but she didn't say anything.

"Hello?"

"Jones, I've been thinking about this, and... If you wouldn't mind letting the family know about Sally. If they want to come in, they can. And if Mom wants to bring the kids, she can. I'm going to give her a ring, but I know the last thing I said was that I wasn't going to, and I just wanted to let you know, so you weren't out of the loop."

"All right. We have to go home and feed the dogs, but we'll be back in."

"I appreciate it. I got to thinking about it, and I honestly don't really want to be alone, and I don't think Sally would want to be either."

"All right. Give us some time, and we'll be back."

"He changed his mind?" Amy said, knowing immediately what had happened as Jones clicked off on his phone.

He nodded. "And he's going to tell your mom that she can bring the kids in if she wants."

"Wow. That's tough."

"Don't they have a horse therapy session scheduled for tomorrow?"

"I think you're right. Maybe… Maybe we can offer to take them in if Mom wants to be with Gilbert."

"Yeah. Whatever he wants. Whatever he wants with them."

"Sure."

It made sense that they would just do whatever it was that he wanted them to do, and they weren't going to insist that they had to do something that was easier for them. It was their job to serve him, since he was the one going through a difficult time.

But that had solidified in Jones's mind what he needed to do.

Chapter Eight

Amy couldn't remember the last time her entire family had been together. Isadora was there, along with her two children. Her husband hadn't made an appearance, but Amy didn't really consider him a part of the family anymore. Not after what he'd done to Isadora. She knew that if he was going to be a part of the children's lives, she might run into him from time to time, and she was going to have to be kind, but it was going to be hard.

Roland was there, standing in the corner with his hands in his pockets. He was probably the one least inclined to have anything to do with it.

For Amy, it brought back thoughts of their dad.

Her mom was beside Sally, holding her hand, Robert on her lap. For once, Robert was still.

Marissa stood beside Amy, holding her hand. Judd and Terry had come in, holding hands, which raised Amy's eyebrows, but she didn't say a word. This wasn't the time or place. She just met Terry's eyes and smiled, giving her an encouraging look.

Terry returned her smile and seemed to have an inquiry of her own on her face. Amy assumed that meant that the idea that she and Jones might be thinking about getting married had made the rounds in the family.

Still, they wouldn't be talking about it here.

Wilson had come, and he stood behind her mom, with Lucas, the oldest of Gilbert's children, standing between Judd and Jones. Lucas called Jones uncle, and Jones had been in their family long enough that he probably felt like a part of it to the young kid.

Everyone was sober, even the children. Gilbert had taken them out and said something to them, and Marissa had come in crying.

Lucas had been stoic, blinking tears away, and Robert just looked a little confused. But sad too.

Like he didn't really understand why his mother had to die.

Maybe that's not what Gilbert told them. She couldn't imagine he could have had anything else to say, since that's what was going to happen.

There was a soft knock on the door, and Amy turned to see Pastor Connelly standing in the doorway.

"Is it okay to come in?" he asked softly.

Gilbert stood up, and the siblings made way for him to move through.

"I'm glad you came, pastor. I appreciate it."

"I'm glad you called me. This is definitely a time to be close to the Lord."

"Sure," Gilbert said, walking back to the bed.

"So the nurse said it was probably going to be tonight?" Pastor Connelly said.

"Yes. Two hours ago, that's what she said. So far, there's been absolutely no change. She hasn't moved at all, except for her breath is maybe getting a little bit rougher. She hasn't woken up."

"Do you mind if I pray?"

"I think we'd all appreciate it if you did," Gilbert said, and Amy wondered what in the world else the pastor would have thought they wanted.

Maybe he was good with bagpipes.

She had to work on not laughing.

Jones's hand came down on her shoulder, like he understood exactly what was going on.

She looked up, a plea for help in her eyes.

He gave her the sternest look he could muster, and she tried to draw from his sobriety.

This was not the time or place for her to be laughing at jokes in her head. She certainly didn't think her sister-in-law's passing was a laughing matter, but she figured the laughter was probably just to ease the stress. She would always much rather laugh than cry. And she also thought if Sally was awake, she would be the first one to say that she would rather have her laughing than crying.

"Lord God, I ask for Your presence to be near us, as our sister in Christ slips into Your arms this evening. I pray Your blessing and peace will be upon us, Your strength give us calmness in our hearts, and in our lives as well, as we realize that she'll be walking the streets of heaven soon and will no longer be in pain, no more cancer, no more scary doctor visits and harsh realities. Everything will be peace and joy and love, as You promise in Your book."

Amy bit back tears. How could she go from laughing to wanting to cry so quickly?

The pastor continued. "Help us to be happy for her, while still grieving the fact that she no longer walks the earth with us. It's right and natural for us to miss her. Your word says that Jesus wept when his friend Lazarus died. It's normal for us to cry. It's normal for us to grieve. You gave us these emotions, and they're not wrong. But, Lord, please help us to move past those emotions, through Your grace and comfort, and rejoin the world of the living, even though the hole that the passing of Sally leaves will forever be in our hearts."

He paused for a moment, and Sally's labored breathing filled the room.

"Help us to grow closer as a family and grow closer to You as Christians. This is not the first time that has happened to this family,

Lord God, and I pray that You bless them, keep them, help them to lean on each other for strength and encouragement in the days ahead. I ask that You give them peace and security and keep them wrapped in Your loving arms. Amen."

No one said anything as the pastor spoke his prayer. Amy fought back tears. Tears of sadness, tears of pain for the children losing their mom. It wasn't much comfort to a child that he should know that their mom was in heaven and happy when they were still on earth and motherless. But God had a plan, and she had to cling tightly to that, because she didn't understand. She never would, but maybe that was because she wasn't God.

Everyone settled in, and no one said much. Even the kids were quiet as they listened to Sally's labored breath.

Then, just before eleven, the sound of her breath changed, it became harsher, not like she was struggling, just a different rhythm, a different sound, which perked Amy up from where she had been standing at the foot of the bed. She was tired and swaying a bit on her feet, but Jones had put his arm around her shoulders, and she leaned into him.

He had been there when her father died, and they grieved together, but that had been years ago, and this was different.

"I think she's leaving us," Gilbert said quietly.

Marissa started crying, Robert was asleep, and no one woke him up, while Lucas stood stoic, his jaw jutted out, his eyes on his mother.

Amy could only imagine what he was thinking, and her heart went out to the little boy who was trying to be a man but was having his mother ripped away from him, and surely his heart was breaking.

Marissa sobbed again, and Amy put her arms around her, drawing her close but allowing her to choose whether she wanted to continue to look at her mom or bury her head in Amy's chest. She chose to continue looking. But her shoulders shook as she did so.

Gilbert looked over at Lucas, and there was a slight change in his face. He lifted his brow, asked a question.

Lucas ran the two steps to his dad and buried his head in his father's neck as Gilbert's arms went around him, and Sally took one last breath and blew it out slowly.

There was no sound in the room, until the monitor gave a long low beep that seemed to go on and on and on.

Maybe they turned it off at the nurse's station, or maybe it turned itself off. Whichever, the room was silent.

Amy swallowed hard. She had been a lot older when her dad died, and it had been hard, but she hadn't been the one who had been left motherless. Which would have been worse. Her dad hadn't been there much at all, and her mom had borne the brunt of raising the children.

It wasn't that she didn't love her dad, because she did, it was just...different. Plus, he had been gone when they had made it to the emergency room, and seeing his lifeless body on the bed, mostly covered with a sheet, had almost seemed surreal.

This brought flashbacks back, and she pressed closer to Jones, putting her arm around him and laying her head against his shoulder.

"Are you okay?" he said so softly she was sure no one else could hear.

She nodded against him.

His hand came up, and it stroked her hair as Marissa turned and buried her face against Amy.

Amy put her arm around Marissa and held her close, stroking her hair, much the same way Jones was comforting her.

Gilbert broke the silence but not with speaking. He began singing "What a Day That Will Be."

Amy had been doing pretty good at not crying, but hearing her brother sing as his wife passed into heaven filled her eyes, and she had to swallow.

Roland and Jones joined him, and soon the whole family was singing.

It was a beautiful heaven song, and she figured that the pastor was right. Maybe there would be tears, but God had a plan. And God had given them a family to lean on during this time. She couldn't think of anything better.

Chapter Nine

$\mathcal{J}$ones dragged himself out of bed in the morning. It had been extremely late, or very early, depending on how one looked at it, before they got to bed last night.

They'd helped Gilbert get his children in the pickup and take them home. Before they left, he'd asked if they would take them to their horse therapy session and spend some time with them while he made arrangements. His mom had said that she would go with him and help him if he needed it.

Of course they'd been happy to say yes, although it was going to be a long day. And perhaps it was going to be a hard day, depending on how the children were taking it.

But he and Amy had a lot of things planned, so they would be busy, because all the things they had planned the children could do with them.

He made two cups of coffee and then got in his truck and headed to Amy's.

Now that he was on to her, he wondered if she would be getting up before him, trying to get into the dog food container and get it done before he saw it.

He figured not, since they hadn't poured the dog food that they bought the day before in the bin; it was still in the back of his truck. So she needed to wait until he got there. He could do it first thing that morning when he got there. Last night, he had dropped her off, made sure she made it into the house okay, and driven directly home.

The last thing he needed or wanted today was an emergency call. He prayed it didn't happen, although Murphy's Law pretty much guaranteed that it would.

Amy stood in the yard, looking at the first rays of sun that were coming over the mountain.

He stopped and got out, grabbing both coffees and walking over. She kept her eyes on the sunrise.

"First sunrise on earth without Sally here," she said softly.

He stopped beside her.

"True," he said, figuring that if she wanted to think like that, that was up to her. He personally wanted to focus on the things that they could do to take care of the children and move on.

But people grieved in different ways, and while Amy wasn't the kind of person who contemplated things for a long time, he knew she could be a deep thinker at times.

Apparently this was one of those times.

"I've never had a sunrise that you haven't been here, somewhere," she said, looking at him.

She had a coat and hat on, and her hair spilled out from underneath her beanie as she held the coffee close to her lips and blew on it but didn't drink any.

"I had four months without you." He grinned. "But I don't remember them."

"Yeah." She turned back and looked at the mountains again. There was pink spilling out from the top of them, although the sun was probably still another thirty minutes from appearing.

Steam drifted out of the holes of their tumblers as they stood looking at the sunrise together.

"Why couldn't we try it?" she said softly, not turning, just staring straight ahead.

He knew immediately what she meant. He had the same thought, maybe brought on because of Sally, maybe seeing Gilbert, maybe knowing that what he had with Amy was special.

"I think we should," he said.

"But not today. Not tomorrow."

"No. We'll have to get a license on Monday. I don't know how long the waiting period is, but I think Friday is thirty days. We need to be married before then."

"All right. Wednesday or Thursday?" she asked, turning and looking at him.

He nodded. "We'll talk to Pastor Connelly."

"I'll invite my family. What about your parents?" She stumbled a bit over the words. They didn't see his parents often, although Amy had seen them almost as much as he had over the past ten years. Because every time he went, he took her with him. Moral support, he supposed.

"I could go today and talk to them and invite them too."

"All right. What about the snowstorm?" she asked, knowing that he was the one who watched the weather out of the two of them.

"Still coming. It said maybe Wednesday."

"So.... Where does that leave us?"

"We get married anytime after we get the license. If we get it Monday. Just find out when the pastor's willing. I guess you'll have a marriage and a funeral this week."

"I think he'll agree to marry us."

"Why wouldn't he?"

"Well, I might wonder if we're actually meaning it. Or for just doing it for the money."

"He wouldn't know anything about the money."

"It's just kinda fast. You know? If I were him, I would be asking questions because I wouldn't want people that I marry to be doing it lightly. And a lot of times, pastors require marriage counseling before a person gets married."

"If he says we have to have marriage counseling, we'll have to see if we can talk about it. Otherwise, we could just get someone at the courthouse to do it. I don't know anything about that, but I'm sure there's such a thing."

"I'm sure you're right."

"I would want this to be a real marriage, and all that entails, for life."

"I know. I got that when we talked yesterday. I want the same thing, I just... I know this is cliché, but I've been up all night thinking about it, and the biggest thing, my biggest fear, is not that we won't make it as a married couple. I know we will. Neither one of us are going to give up. I just... I don't want to lose our friendship."

She turned as she said that and looked up at him, and his heart melted. How could it not? The thing that she was the most concerned about was not herself, not the money, not whether she was doing the right thing, it was him. His friendship with her. He meant that much to her.

"I don't think it's cliché, because it's true. Sometimes when friends try to be more, everything blows up in their face. I've seen it happen, and I know you have too."

"I have," she said, nodding.

"Then we'll just have to make sure we don't let that happen. I can't imagine being mad at you, although I know it's possible."

"You did get mad at me once a few years ago."

"It's been ten years since, and I was justified in my anger at the time."

"I didn't think you were," she said, lifting a shoulder like she had nothing to do with it.

"Stop right there, missy. You were just as mad as I was, and you didn't talk to me for three whole hours, which to you is a lifetime."

He had his finger up, and he pointed at her.

"You're ruining the sunrise with a raised voice," she said,

grabbing his finger, and he braced himself, because had it been someone else, they would have bent it back or something, but she took it, brought his hand up and linked his arm with hers, then slid her fingers together.

"A real marriage," she said, looking at their hands.

She took a breath and closed her eyes, blowing it out slowly. "That kiss yesterday changed my mind about a lot of things."

"Same. And it wasn't even that good."

Her eyes popped open, and her head jerked to his. "Not that good?"

"I'm pretty sure we will have better ones in the near future," he said, one side of his mouth turning up.

Her lips quirked too. "Okay. I'll give you that."

They stared at the sunrise, watching as the sky grew pinker and brighter with spots of orange and light blue as day broke.

She was right, it was their first day without Sally. Lucas, Marissa, and Robert's first day without their mother. And it was the first day of a new turn in the relationship that he had with Amy. He stood there thinking about it all, along with the new start with his best friend, her hand in his, as the sun rose, the brightness of the sunrise bloomed and then faded, and the sky turned milky blue.

"We have a lot of things to do today."

"Are we still going to bake cookies?"

"I kinda think the kids would enjoy helping us. We can do that at your mom's. We should make it there before they get up."

"And then we're taking them with us as we visit the kids we'll be picking up in the horse-drawn wagon tomorrow, right?"

"Right, and then at two o'clock, they have their horse therapy session."

"And after that, we're dropping them off with someone else and taking a nap."

"Or planning our wedding."

She laughed. "What do we have to plan? I mean, it's not going to be fancy or anything, right? Do I need to go dress shopping? You saw how much money was in my bank account, right?"

"You saw how much money I was inheriting, right?"

Her laughter carried on the breeze as they turned and walked toward the dog kennels.

"You know that's our money."

"I had no doubt of it, although isn't money the number one thing that couples fight about?"

"I think so. What are you trying to say? That we can't have money or we'll fight?" He huffed out a breath and grunted. "You think I have to give it away? Or not claim it?"

"That's up to you."

"No. It's up to us," he said, holding her hand up, their fingers laced together, the sight unfamiliar. This was new. This whole relationship thing. He wasn't quite sure where it was going to take them, but he knew for sure that wherever it was, he wanted Amy beside him.

Chapter Ten

"*L*ook at this!" Marissa said as she held up the gingerbread man that she just decorated. For nine years old, Amy thought she had done a great job. Probably better than Amy could do since she had absolutely no artistic ability at all.

Jones, on the other hand, had decorated three different gingerbread men, one with a suit and tie, one dressed as an astronaut, of all things, and one who looked like a typical gingerbread man.

Robert seemed to be doing the best, and Marissa was enjoying it, although she had times of sadness and once had broken out in tears.

Lucas was quiet, pensive, and didn't join in a lot of their conversations, but he had helped make the batter, roll it out, and cut out the gingerbread men, and now he was mixing up the molasses cookies with Amy.

"You can crack those eggs, and we're ready to put them in now. Make sure you don't get any shells in them," she said.

"Aunt Amy, aren't you going to decorate a gingerbread man?" Marissa asked, looking up from the one that she sat in front of.

"My gingerbread men look hideous. They look like ballerinas or something," she said, trying to figure what in the world could be the most hideous thing a gingerbread person could possibly look like.

"That's a good idea!" Marissa said. "This one's going to be a ballerina."

Well, the church kids were going to be shocked when they showed up at their house handing out gingerbread men ballerinas.

Hopefully that wouldn't affect the taste, so maybe it would be okay.

Jones met her eyes over the heads of the kids, and they shared a little smile.

He knew how she felt about her ability to decorate, and that's why he had taken the lead there. She could mix things up and cook them to perfection, and if she had had a choice, they would have made just regular cookies. But they thought that the kids would enjoy the decorations, and they'd been right.

She hadn't heard anything out of her mom and Gilbert, and she hoped everything was going well.

"When I was a kid, my parents didn't cook with me like this, so it's good that you have an aunt who takes the time to do that," Jones said as he picked up another gingerbread man and started squeezing some icing from the tube on him.

"Aunt Amy's always done it. But you've always been there too," Marissa said, and then she looked up, thoughtful. "Are you going to be our parents now?"

Her lips trembled, and her eyes filled with tears.

Amy wasn't far from her, so she nodded at Lucas who was pouring the eggs in and took a step to put her arm around Marissa.

"Your dad will still be your parent, honey." She couldn't promise everything would be the same, because it wouldn't be.

"I just want Mom to come back," she said, her tears spilling down her cheeks until she buried her head against Amy, like she had the night before.

Amy knew that today was probably going to be hard for everyone, and the cookies were just a Band-Aid.

It would take them a while to work through their grief. Although, she felt like with the right, positive direction, they would be able to have a good frame around which to put their thoughts. The idea that God was good might be a little bit hard to swallow, and she was a little concerned for the children.

She didn't want them to be angry at Him, so she hesitated to bring Him up at all.

"Me too!" Robert said, dropping his icing and running over to put his arms around Amy.

Jones stood. She knew that this was not something he was comfortable with. That he would rather be far, far away, but he came over to where she stood with the two kids.

"You might as well join the group hug, Lucas," Jones said, wrapping his arms around Marissa and Robert.

"I don't like crying," he said, but he put the spoon in the batter and came over.

"I think maybe your siblings just need you to be here right now. You don't have to cry," Jones said.

"I don't think it's fair. Why does it have to be us to lose our mom? Why can't it be...someone else."

So different than the boy he was even a week ago, two weeks ago, when he volunteered to use the leaf blower with Judd.

But that was how quickly things could turn in a person's mind. Of course, there was a lot of changes since then, and his mom was no longer with them. At the time, no one had realized that she had less than two weeks to live.

"God gives us all trials we have to get through," Amy started, not sure where she was going with that.

"And our trials make us stronger. The harder the trials, the stronger we can get, but we have to lean on the Lord and realize that whatever He does, He's got a plan, and it's for our good."

"This doesn't feel good. How can death be good?"

"What makes you think it's bad?" Jones said.

"Because my mom isn't here anymore?" Lucas said, like it was obvious.

"But she's in heaven. That's better than here. And when you get to heaven, she'll be right there waiting to greet you. You've got someone waiting for you in heaven right now, and you don't have to worry about dying, like…sometimes you're scared, right? At least I am, of dying," she said. "But after my dad died, I started thinking that he did it, why can't I? And if he did it, and he's a Christian and he's in heaven, he's waiting on me. So, there's Jesus, too, but when I was little, I worried that I wouldn't recognize him."

"But I think we will recognize him. I think we just automatically will," Jones said.

"I think you might be right. But when I was little, I was scared I wouldn't. But after Dad died, I wasn't afraid to die anymore, because I knew I would have someone I knew in heaven. So I can just run right to my dad, and he'll take me to his house, he'll introduce me to all his friends, and we'll just hang out there and wait for the rest of the family to get there."

"But what about me? I'm still here?"

"That's right. And so, you keep your mom's memory in mind, and you remember the things that she taught you, and you do your best to grow up to be the man that she wanted you to be. Didn't she tell you that you needed to love Jesus?"

"Yeah."

"What else did she tell you you need to do?"

"She told me I was supposed to take care of Dad and my siblings. But I'm only twelve!"

"Some of us grow up early," Jones said. "But I'm sure she didn't mean that you are supposed to get a job and provide for them. She just meant, don't fight with them. Be nice to them, learn to get along with them, because she loves them, she loves you, and she wanted you all to get along."

Amy had not signed up for this counseling of children with grief, and she wasn't sure that she was saying anything right. She hoped she was saying something that would help not hinder, but she felt entirely inadequate for the situation.

But she looked over Lucas's head at Jones, he smiled at her, and it made her feel like maybe she wasn't doing such a terrible job.

"I just want her to come back."

"She's not coming back to you, but you can go to her, when it's your turn to go. It's like I told Lucas, she'll be there waiting for you, but there's no rush to get there. You need to be here and grow up. Live your life."

"She doesn't get to see it! What's the point?" Lucas said.

"How do you know she doesn't see it?" Amy said. Although she believed in spirits, she didn't believe that spirits people could see were from the Lord. She did, however, believe that a person's life would eventually be on display for anyone to see, since the Bible said that all the hidden things would be revealed. She was certainly willing to say that she could be wrong about that, since she didn't exactly know how they would be revealed, but it stood to reason that God wouldn't deprive a mother of being able to see her children grow up.

There was always the idea, though, that once a person got to heaven, they didn't really care anymore about what went on on earth. Because they would be so interested in seeing and praising Jesus.

"I guess I don't," Marissa said, seeming thoughtful.

"I don't know whether she can or not, but I guess, I would live my life like she could, just in case. After all, if you get to heaven and find out she couldn't, you've lived a good life. But if you get to heaven and find out she could, and you didn't live like it, then you've probably got some problems, because your mom's not going to be very happy with you."

Lucas actually almost smiled, his lips trembled anyway, and Marissa seemed to be drying her tears.

"Can I go back and decorate my gingerbread man?" she asked.

"You sure can."

"We were going to take these and give them to the kids who ride in the wagon with us to church. You guys are welcome to come. Or if you don't want to, one of us can stay home, and only one of us will go." Jones looked at Amy, with his brows raised, as if asking if that was okay.

She nodded. Of course it was. She wasn't going to quibble over details. And she also figured that some of the kids might want to go, and maybe not all the kids would want to go.

"You're going to go visiting?" Robert asked tentatively.

"We sure are," Jones said, ruffling his hair before he walked back around the bar and sat back down in front of his gingerbread man.

"We can go?" Marissa said.

"If you want to," Amy said, walking over and watching as Lucas stirred the cookies.

"I want to go. I want to be able to tell them that I did it."

"You certainly can. You've done the lion's share of the work."

"I want to, too!" Marissa said.

"Me too!" Robert added.

"You guys have all been a great help. It's only right that you get to go deliver them and tell people that you made them if you want to. You can even decorate certain cookies for certain people, although you have to be nice about it," Jones said, adding that last bit just in case the kids got any ideas about being funny.

They seemed interested, and they talked about who they were decorating their cookies for, while Lucas finished mixing up the molasses cookies and they started baking them.

The kids were struggling, sure, but it was to be expected, since they lost their mom the day before. Hopefully, doing all this would get their mind off things.

"And after we go visiting, we'll be doing your horseback riding therapy, which you've done for two weeks," she said, knowing that the kids loved it.

"Both today!" Robert said, jumping up. "Yay! I hope I get to ride Boomer. He was the best horse she had."

"No. My horse was the best horse," Lucas said, turning around to stick his tongue out at his brother.

Amy was tempted to tell him that she didn't think that was what his mother meant when she told him to take care of his siblings, but she didn't want to put too much pressure on his young shoulders, so she clamped her mouth closed. He would probably be hearing that a good bit over his lifetime, and she didn't need to start the chorus today.

"My horse, Princess Buttercup, was the best horse. She's the best because she's a princess," Marissa said, stating it like it was a fact.

"She's not a princess," Lucas said.

"Yes, she is. It's in her name. And on her papers. They told me she was registered as Princess Buttercup."

Jones and Amy exchanged glances again.

This time, there was still sadness in their eyes as they looked at each other, but there was a smile there too.

"What do you think about taking Mocha on the wagon on Sunday?" Amy said, the idea coming to her on the spur of the moment.

She watched Jones's face.

The kids all cheered, because they loved Mocha, although she hadn't brought her today since they were baking cookies.

"That may be a good way to get her adopted, if you have her on the wagon where everyone can see her."

"I was thinking that, but mostly I was just thinking that she would love it, and the kids might enjoy it as well."

"We can dress her like a reindeer!" Marissa said excitedly.

Amy didn't do too much of that kind of stuff for Christmas, especially at church, because she wanted to be sure that they were celebrating Christmas and not mixing secularism in with what should have been the holiest day of the year. Other than possibly Easter.

"We can do that," she said, not wanting to split hairs with something that got Marissa so happy. She supposed there would be time enough to be clear about what Christmas was about and what it wasn't.

Although, over the years, Christmas would probably be hard, after losing their mom right around the holidays.

"Can I hold her?" Marissa asked.

"Sure. She'd probably really like that."

They talked a little more about the kids in the wagon and how they were going to be delivering cookies later, when Amy's phone buzzed.

She met Jones's eyes, touched her pocket where it was, and then walked out of the kitchen.

She pulled it out of her pocket and swiped on.

"Hello?" she said, standing in the hall, tempted to walk into the bathroom.

"Amy, how are the kids?" Her mom's voice came over the phone.

"They're doing fine. They had a couple of times where they've cried, but right now, they're talking about taking Mocha on the wagon when we pick the kids up for church, and they're pretty excited about that."

"And the cookies?"

"I think they're going to go with us later to deliver them. They were excited that they could decorate certain cookies for certain kids, although it might make visitation last twice as long as what it usually does." She could just imagine each kid going, "where is the cookie that I decorated for you," and going through every one of them trying to remember. It had the makings of a nightmare, but it would keep the kids thinking about something else while time did its work. And God healed their hearts.

"I'm glad to hear it. Gilbert is...doing fine. I guess. He's kind of unemotional. And that worries me as much as if he were inconsolable."

"He's a man." She knew men cried. It wasn't a secret or anything, but they tried harder than women not to. Although, she figured if someone lost their wife, they should be given a pass on the whole not crying thing.

"I know. Well, we've made the arrangements for the funeral, we talked to the pastor, and we checked the weather. We thought we'd better wait until after the storm passes, so the funeral is going to be Friday. We knew that both Terry and Jones have Friday off. I know it's going to be the Friday before Christmas, but... It is what it is."

"That's fine. That's probably best."

"All right. I wanted to let you know. We're on our way home. I suppose the kids can decide at that point whether they want to go with you, or whether they want to stay home."

"That's fine. We told them they could choose, and if you guys weren't back, one of us was going to stay."

"All right."

"Also, don't forget about their horse therapy at two."

"Oh. I had forgotten. I'll remind Gilbert."

"All right. Mom, I put a casserole in the fridge, so you don't have to worry about it, and then three different ladies from church showed up with food, so there's plenty to eat here. Just to let you know."

"Thank you. I don't think either one of us are hungry, but I have yet to see Gilbert where he truly couldn't eat, so that's good to know."

"Yeah. I just wanted to let you know you didn't have to worry about cooking anything."

"Thanks. And I know he really appreciates you and Jones taking care of the kids."

"Not a problem. Terry said Judd had some things he had to do, but she was happy to stop in, so she's available too."

"I really appreciate the way you all are pitching in. It's nice to have a family."

"It sure is."

Chapter Eleven

Gilbert stared at the casket that would soon hold his wife. His mother had been awesome. Beside him, supporting him, but not interfering unless he asked.

He had wanted to have a special kind of relationship with Sally, but she had been always running ahead of him. Demanding her own way and getting angry if he didn't comply with her every wish.

He shouldn't have married her. He had been deeply attracted to her, infatuated with her, and had not seen how different they actually were. How incompatible. Or maybe he just hadn't seen her true personality. The selfishness she displayed, her need to have all of the attention focused on herself. Her lack of character.

He still remembered the letter that she'd gotten almost exactly four years prior.

He'd been opening the mail, and hadn't even noticed that it was addressed only to her, but had gone ahead and opened it, without thinking. After all, he didn't think there were any secrets in his marriage.

Boy, had he been wrong.

Taking a deep breath, he walked to the window in the small room that held the caskets for display.

He'd never been in a room like this. Were all funeral parlors like this? He didn't know. He'd never been involved in the choosing of the casket. The intimate details of the funeral. Which pen would you like to use? What stationery would you like?

He didn't want anything fancy. He didn't want a big show. It wasn't because of Sally and the letter. Wasn't because of what the letter contained or how that had changed his life, irrevocably.

They'd worked it out. He'd forgiven her, but he'd never trusted her again.

Maybe they wouldn't have worked it out if it hadn't been for his children. But he couldn't look at his kids and not try. No matter how badly his own heart had broken.

Now, it was like all of that work had gone down the tubes, because he still ended up a single dad with three children.

Lord, how am I going to raise them on my own?

He had done as much work as Sally had with the kids, maybe even more. She'd taken girls' days, spa days, PMS days, and had spent weeks at a time at her mother's house especially when the children were small, and the work was never ending.

He picked up the slack, his mom had watched the kids any time he asked, and he'd been there with them every minute he wasn't working.

He stared without seeing out the glass, thinking about how he'd wanted to have a marriage like God commanded. That had been his goal from the time he was young. But maybe he'd gotten caught up in seeing how a woman looked, her hair, her face, the curve of her waist, the flare of her hips, and more. Sally had that all. She hadn't lost it with three children, either. She was just as trim now as she had been the day they were married. Oh, she did say she gained weight, and maybe she had, but she was still beautiful, fit, and trim. Of course, she went to the gym three times a week religiously.

He often wondered if maybe there was something going on there.

He hadn't thought anything like that before the letter, then after, he'd wondered. Were there more?

He supposed part of the fault was his. He had trouble being interested in his wife since he found out she'd been unfaithful. He tried. She apologized, and he forgave her, and they'd gone to some counseling sessions, but she refused to take responsibility and blamed him for the most part. Maybe it was his fault. He felt like he twisted himself into pretzels trying to be the man that she wanted him to be, and he always came up short.

Did that make everything his fault?

Or was she too demanding? Her standards too impossible to meet, her desire to be loved by everyone overcoming her ability to stay faithful.

Sometimes he looked at Robert and wondered if he was really his.

He sighed, blowing out a breath and then walking from the window back over to the casket that he'd chosen. All of them were fine; he didn't care. The funeral was going to be expensive, and it was going to wipe out the small amount of savings he had. He hadn't chosen the cheapest casket, but he'd chosen this one, which had a few little fancy things on it that he thought that Sally would probably like. Even thought he'd long ago stopped caring what she liked, he made himself go through the motions. She wasn't all that interested in him, and it didn't seem to matter what he did, he couldn't recapture that. She had told him that he had changed, that he wasn't fun, that he was too wrapped up in his family and he ran to them any time they needed help, so he'd gotten to the point where he pretty much didn't do anything with his family at all. He'd given it all up, and still she wasn't happy.

And yet, who was here for her when Sally had gotten sick?

His family—his sisters, his mom, they surrounded him, helped with his children, cooked them meals, washed his clothes, cleaned his house. He noticed and had been thankful. Meanwhile, Sally's mom had come a couple of times, then taken him aside and admitted that she hated to see her daughter suffer so badly, and she wouldn't be able to help.

He texted her the day Sally died and told her that it would probably be her last chance to see her daughter alive.

It had taken a while for her to text back, and she told him that she would prefer to just remember her the way she last saw her. And then she gave him a warning, saying that was the way the children would prefer as well.

It had made him doubt himself, especially since Sally had said the same thing.

Seeing her sick hadn't made it so that he didn't remember her when she was well. It had made it so that he understood just how bad she was suffering. And whether there was love or hate in his heart, he couldn't not be compassionate when a fellow human was suffering.

Lord, I don't want to tell everyone what I know about her. I don't want them to hate her, to think less of her, and I definitely don't want her children to think that either.

Should he continue to hide it? Should he ever tell them?

He didn't know. He'd kept the secret for years, because she'd repented to him and apologized, and he didn't think she deserved to have her name dragged through the mud, just so that everyone could know how badly he had suffered.

Was he making the right choice?

He often doubted that. He envied the men who seemed to have it all together, who seemed to make decisions without thought, snap decisions that always turned out to be the right ones.

Of course, people might look at him and think he made decisions without struggling with them, but they would be so, so wrong.

He breathed out heavily again and hooked a hand behind his neck, shoving his other hand in his pocket as he walked to the coffin. It would be this one. The funeral director had told him so. That they would be taking it out of the showroom later.

He would prefer to see pictures. Prefer to choose it out of a catalog. That made it less real.

But it wouldn't have made it less necessary for him to go through it all. He was her husband. He had to be there. He had to be a father to his children and somehow figure out where he was going to go from here, what he was going to do. One thing he knew, he owed a debt of gratitude to his family.

A second thing he was pretty sure of. He would never trust another woman. Or maybe, he would never trust himself to choose another wife. He'd obviously made a big mistake, and he didn't intend to do it again.

Chapter Twelve

"Look how beautiful these cookies are!" Amy said as she admired the gingerbread men they'd individually wrapped and the molasses cookies that Lucas had baked, allowed to cool, and then dipped in white chocolate with his siblings.

"We can sell these at a bakeshop or something," Jones said, admiring the bagged gingerbread men.

He had closed the end and put the ribbon around it. Amy would have messed that up, but she could get the gingerbread man in without breaking him. The kids had been a huge help, and they eagerly stood around watching as Amy and Jones admired their handiwork.

There was still sadness, and she knew that there were going to be more tears, but it had been a good idea to go ahead and continue with what they had planned. Kids were different than adults, although she thought grief came in waves for everyone. That's how it had been for her with her dad. One second, she was perfectly fine, and the next second, she'd been hit with a wave of grief so hard she was crying before she knew what happened. And then, without rhyme or reason, it was over and she was fine again.

"So are we ready to go?" she asked, looking around at the kids, who nodded eagerly, before she glanced at Jones.

"We'll have to take your car, because I think the cookies will fit better in your trunk, and the kids can all fit in the back."

"That's fine. You want to go get it?"

She had just asked that when the door opened, and she glanced up.

Her sister, Isadora, a baby on one hip, pregnant stomach protruding, and another toddler holding her hand, pushed through.

"Isadora!" Amy said, running to the door to open it and to take Landon off her hip.

"I'm sorry. I know that this is the worst possible time. Gilbert is going through things, and it's almost Christmas, and I'm sorry," she said, tears running down her face, as she gladly handed Landon off to Amy.

"I'll tell you what. You stay here with Isadora, the kids and I will go deliver cookies. We won't have to switch vehicles that way. We'll do the visiting. Okay?" Jones said as he came over, putting a hand on Amy's shoulder. He knew immediately what was going on, because he knew that Isadora had been having issues with her husband, and this had to be related to that.

"Thank you," she breathed, looking up at him, with such relief and appreciation in her heart she could hardly contain herself. Isadora needed her. She wished she could have been there more for her, but no one had really realized what was going on until earlier in the week.

"No. Whatever you're doing, you don't have to stop," Isadora said, swiping at her face and waving a tear off as another one rolled down immediately and took its place.

"I'm sure you're fine, but I'm going to be here for you anyway. Mom's with Gilbert, and Jones can take care of the visiting."

"The kids are going to have a good time. We've got some

beautiful cookies to deliver," Jones said easily. Then he looked at Amy. "I'll text you before I go to horse therapy, to see if you want to come."

"Perfect. I'll be in touch," she said, figuring that she would text Jones as soon as she was done talking to Isadora, unless there was more to do. And there probably was. After all, someone was going to have to take care of the little ones, but thankfully there was food in the refrigerator and more had come in earlier. Who had known that they would be needing it so much?

Landon grabbed a hold of her hair and pulled, but Amy ignored the pain.

"Do you need help carrying the cookies out?" she asked as Isadora came over and started taking Jasper's coat off, wiping her eyes and sniffling as she did so.

"I can help!" Lucas said, stepping forward eagerly.

"You've done an excellent job today. I trust you to carry the cookies. Which ones do you want?" And Jones took it from there.

Amy could have kissed him, and the thought didn't even make her shudder and wonder what was wrong with her, why she would be wanting to kiss her best friend. The idea wasn't...terrible. In fact, it might have been kind of...nice.

But maybe it was an idea she had to get used to. She had Landon's coat off, which was no small feat since Landon had not started walking yet so she had to sit him down on the floor, and pull it off, and then make sure he didn't crawl away and get into something while she was hanging it up.

She came back and grabbed him just before he toppled the garbage can.

He was fast. She couldn't imagine trying to take care of such a speedy little guy and nurse a broken heart, pregnant at the same time.

"I'm so sorry that you missed visitation and whatever else you and Jones were doing," Isadora said as she sniffed, walking over to the counter and grabbing a tissue out of the box, still keeping one eye on Jasper, who was two, almost three, but still needed to be watched so that he didn't get into anything he wasn't supposed to. "But Jones is such a great friend. He's always picking up for you, or you're picking up for him. I've never seen two people who flowed together the way you two do, and yet you're water and oil."

That was kind of nice, but water and oil didn't mix? She wanted to ask Isadora exactly what she meant by that.

"Actually, that's a really great analogy, because you guys don't mix. You don't lose your identities, but you flow together perfectly." Her voice trailed off, and then her eyes filled with tears again, and she leaned her head back, as though trying to stop herself. "He told me yesterday that he was going to come back. We could work things out, he loved me, and that he wanted the children, and then... She must have called him overnight, because this morning, I woke up and he was packing suitcases."

"He's a jerk. He is such a jerk," Amy said, wanting to say stronger words. Surely it was okay to use stronger words when a person was talking about someone who would leave his pregnant wife and two small children.

"I know. I know he is. He was never very considerate, and I always ended up doing the lion's share for everything, and... I just wanted my marriage to work. You know? Like if I put enough time and effort into it, I could make it work all by myself, when I knew very well that it takes two."

"Well, it might have worked. If he hadn't cheated. It's not a fun way to live, but when you have to keep your vows, you do what you need to do."

"Yeah. That's exactly right."

Amy didn't know what Isadora had been through, but she knew that Isadora was as faithful as a person could be. That even after her husband cheated on her, Isadora would have stayed with him, just because her vows meant something to her, and having a home with a mom and dad in it for her children was paramount. More important than anything.

Amy set Landon down by the toy box and went over, putting her arms around Isadora, and just held her while she sobbed.

She kept an eye on Landon and Jasper, making sure they didn't get into anything that would hurt them, while she held their mom. Her sobs crescendoed, then slowly subsided.

"Do you want to talk?" Amy asked, not knowing how she would feel in this situation. Would she want to talk and get it off her chest? Or would she want to hide in a cave somewhere? Would she want to fix everything right away? Move out and start a new life or figure out how she could get things set up so she felt like she was in control?

"I think it would make me feel better. I've been by myself for so long."

"He didn't really want you to see us, did he?" Amy asked, hesitantly, because she was not a hundred-percent sure about that, but it did seem like Clyde had deliberately tried to keep Isadora away from everyone in her family.

"He preferred not. And I just wanted to make him happy. I took care of the kids, but it felt like I was a single mom, because he continued to do all the things that he had done before we were married, before we had children, before...before."

She moved to the couch and sat down on the edge of it, her elbows on her knees, her head in her hands.

Amy sat down beside her, putting her arm around her and allowing her to lean into her if she chose.

"I just feel like such a fool!"

"I think everyone was deceived by Clyde. He's a very smooth talker. And the woman that he's with now must be deceived by him. Does she even know that Clyde has a family? Children?"

"I don't know. I don't even know who it is. He wouldn't tell me."

Amy wondered whether she should tell her sister that she had seen a picture on social media with Clyde and another woman the day before. She wasn't on social media much, and when she'd seen that, she clicked it back off.

She didn't remember where she'd seen it.

"It probably doesn't matter. I guess. I just... I feel worthless, you know? Like I'm a broodmare, and he doesn't even want my babies anymore."

"That's on him. That's a character thing on him. And no. You're beautiful, athletic, and happy, but more than the outside, you have character. You have loyalty. You have the ability to make promises and keep them. You have the ability to tell yourself no and do the right thing, even when it's hard. Even when you want to do something else."

Amy thought again about how she had wanted to use foul language describing Clyde, but she hadn't allowed herself to do it. It was those little things. The little things where a person controlled their language, controlled their thoughts, they controlled what time they get up in the morning, and that translated into being able to control oneself for the bigger things. When you were tempted to stray from your marriage, when you were tempted to cheat or to lie.

That, and depending on the Lord to help you, doing things in His strength rather than your own.

"I appreciate your kind words. I don't feel very appealing right now at the moment. It doesn't help that I'm pregnant, and I feel clumsy and stupid, stupid, stupid for believing him when he said he wanted to have a lot of children and close together so that they could all be best friends growing up."

She started to cry again, and Amy put her arm around her. Wishing there was something she could do to help.

"Do you mind watching the kids for a little bit? I just want to go lie down and curl up on the bed in the dark and be alone."

Her voice sounded so defeated, so hopeless, so exhausted, that Amy couldn't do anything but agree.

"The kids will be fine. I'll take care of them. Just give me a few ideas of where they're at. Landon has gotten a lot faster since the last time I saw him."

That made Isadora laugh a little, through her tears, and she said, "Yeah. He'll take anything and put it in his mouth, so you have to watch that. And Jasper's really good at helping to keep an eye on him. They both take naps in the afternoon, usually around one, and sometimes Landon still takes a morning nap, but if he doesn't get up before nine, I try not to let him take a nap because he won't sleep in the afternoon."

"All right. I think I have it. You take all the time you need. If you want to go to my house where you can have some privacy, you can do that. Or whatever. If you end up there, just let me know, and I'll bunk down here or do something. I'll be around to feed the dogs, but I don't need to go into the house."

She thought about all the things that she and Jones were planning and wondered if she could manage to do everything without even being in her house, and where were they going to live after they were married?

There were so many questions in her own life, and now this with her sister, and she tried to steel her mind, to relax in God's provision and care. He had this all arranged, He knew exactly what was going to happen, and she didn't need to get excited about it. She didn't need to get worried, and she didn't need to get flustered.

She didn't need to get angry either, but she kind of figured that even God would get angry at what Clyde had done.

"Could I really go to your house? I would love just to be alone. Just alone," Isadora said, and Amy was heartbroken. Isadora had been such a vivacious, cheerful, happy teen. And she'd made one bad choice. Just one. And it had broken her.

"Of course. Spend as much time as you need to there."

"All right. I'm going to take the car seats out of my car, just in case you need to take them anywhere."

Amy didn't bother to tell her that she didn't have a vehicle, since her mom was gone and she had ridden in with Jones. But she supposed someone would be back, and the car seats would fit in anyone's car.

"All right. I appreciate it. Just set them on the driveway, and when I put the kids down for their naps, I'll go out and get them and bring them in."

"Thank you so much. I appreciate it."

"No problem. If there's anything I can do, anything at all, just let me know. We've got plenty of food here, but I'm guessing you're probably not hungry." She knew that she probably wouldn't be able to eat. Even though there weren't too many times in her life where she'd been that upset. But having her husband cheat on her and then pack a suitcase as she's pregnant, with two small children running around, yeah. That would probably throw anyone off their appetite.

"You're right. I don't have any interest in food at all. Thank you." And for some reason, that made Isadora's eyes fill up with tears again as she stood from the couch and wrapped her arms around Amy who stood with her. "I'm so sorry. I want to be a good mom, I want to be able to parent my children, but this pain, it's just so crushing," she said, her voice sounding like it hurt to even talk.

"Give yourself some time. You're going to be a good mom. But the pain is inhibiting, and you just need to give yourself a little bit of time, to let the sharpness of the pain wear off, and you will be a good mom. You will. But you had such a huge blow. You need to give your body and your emotions a little bit of time to at least come to grips with this." Amy gave a gentle smile, pulling back and trying to get Isadora to meet her eyes. "If you had a broken leg, you wouldn't expect to walk on it right away? Right?"

Isadora swiped her eyes, nodding.

"It's the same thing here. You need time. You might have to live broken, but you don't have to do it today."

"Thank you. Thank you so much," Isadora said, and then she kissed each of her little boys. Landon swiped her face with his chubby hands but didn't protest when she set him back down. But Jasper tried to cling to his mom, seeming to realize that she was going to be leaving him, and he already had his little world interrupted and turned upside down.

"Jasper, it's okay. It's Aunt Amy. We're going to play some, and then I bet you're hungry. We made cookies today, and a cookie might be just the thing," she said, thinking that if they were her kids, she would be perfectly happy with anyone feeding them anything at all if it made them happy. Maybe tomorrow, when things weren't so dire, would be time to be a little bit more strict about junk food, but today, bribes seemed to be in order.

Jasper didn't seem the slightest bit interested in a bribe and held his hands out for his mom who walked out the door.

She was back in just a moment later and said, "Here's the baby bags. I'm sorry. There's sippy cups and snacks and diapers and stuff like that in there." She let out a big sigh, like it had been all she could do to carry the diaper bags in.

"Go lie down. Take care of yourself. I'll text you with updates, but don't feel like you need to respond. If I have any questions, I'll ask. Otherwise, just focus on you for now."

She didn't know what else to say to her. Didn't know what else to do. How else to help. Other than what she was doing.

"Thank you," Isadora said, once more walking out.

By now, Jasper was crying, almost inconsolably, and Landon, seeing his brother cry, had started to cry too. She was tired. They'd been up early after sleeping very little, after watching her sister-in-law die and her nephews and nieces lose their mother, and she felt a little bit like crying herself.

She could do this. She'd offered help, and she would do her best. She just had to try to figure out what she was going to do. Probably first, she should figure out how to get the kids to stop crying.

Chapter Thirteen

"I had fun shopping with you. I think the Secret Saint thing is going to be much better with you beside me," Judd said as he and Terry put their groceries in the car and then put the cart in the cart return.

"I can definitely get into it. There are so many people who need to be helped and so many ways that my eyes have been opened since I started even thinking about it. I guess people just don't think, you know?"

Judd nodded. And Terry's heart swelled. There weren't a lot of people who would look at Judd and think that he had a whole lot to teach someone like her, and she wasn't thinking that arrogantly, it was just the truth. But he'd been instrumental in helping her see things that she never had before. Not to mention, he was a man of character and she loved him.

Christmas music blared out of the speakers into the parking lot, and the Christmas decorations along the pole lights at the end of the parking lot glittered in the daylight.

Judd opened her car door. "I don't think it would be overstating things to say that you're the best thing that ever happened to me."

He grinned, and she paused, and rather than sitting down in the car, she put her hand on his cheek and kissed the side of his lips.

"I could say the exact same thing."

They smiled at each other, and then she said, "I was going to tell my family tomorrow?"

"That's fine with me. I know losing your sister-in-law was a big blow, and Gilbert is probably reeling right now."

"I know. I just don't want to wait too long. We're not living together, exactly, but—"

"It doesn't look the greatest, I agree. I don't want it to look like something's going on that isn't. So let's just make it official, and then we won't have to worry about that."

She nodded, knowing for a certainty that that was the right choice, and that other people might say that she was rushing into things, but she knew the kind of person Judd was, and she knew herself as well. Neither one of them were going to be looking for an escape hatch or taking the easy way out. They were in it for life, and with God's blessing, they would make it work.

She reluctantly dropped her hands and sat down in the seat, while he closed the door behind her, walking around to the other side.

She waited until he had gotten in and started the car, and they were pulling out of the parking lot. "Do you mind dropping me off at my family's house? It's not that I don't want to help you deliver these..."

"No. I know that things have been kind of unsettled there lately, and you feel pulled to help. As much as I want to spend all of my waking hours with you, and all of your off-duty hours, I understand."

"All right. I appreciate that," she said as he pulled out onto the highway, and they started toward her mother's house.

She couldn't believe the way her life had changed so crazily in just a month. But even harder things had happened to her family, and now that she was home, she wanted to be there for them.

They chatted a bit, until he got to her mother's house and pulled in.

"You don't have to get out unless you want to. It doesn't look like there's anyone here, but there's a light on inside."

"You want me to wait?"

"No. You go on. I'll text you if it turns out that someone just forgot to shut it off."

"All right. I love you," he said, and she leaned across her seat toward him and kissed him. Wishing she didn't have to get out, didn't have to leave, could sit here and just spend the entire day with him. But it wasn't very often that a person actually got to do exactly what they wanted to. And that was probably for the best.

She pulled the latch and got out of the car.

Almost immediately, she could hear crying. No, it sounded like screaming. From a little child.

She waved as Judd drove away and saw his hand go up in return. Then, she turned toward the house and rushed up the walk. Whatever was going on inside, she was a part of this family, and she was going to help if she could.

Opening the door, she saw Amy standing in the dining room, hand on one hip, Jasper crying at her feet. She was in the process of kneeling down, probably to talk to Jasper. She ended up picking up Landon and pulling Jasper toward her.

Neither one of the boys had stopped crying, and it looked a little bit like Amy was going to start crying too.

Amy must have seen movement, because she certainly couldn't have heard the door open over all of the wailing that was going on, but her head lifted up, and the relief that stole across her face was unmistakable.

"I am so happy to see you. Please tell me you're here to stay, for at least, I don't know, until he stops crying?" she said, her words a little bit funny, but her need for help obvious.

"I'm here. To stay. As long as you need me today. I want to talk to you anyway."

"Perfect! Would you mind bringing the diaper bag over? Isadora said there were diapers in there, and I think this little guy needs to be changed."

They were talking loudly to be heard over the crying, but even though the children probably had good reason to cry, Terry knew they wouldn't cry forever.

Eventually they would stop, even if nothing was done. But they could do their very best to try to help them. And of course they would.

She set the diaper bag down and scooped up Jasper.

"What are you doing, little guy? Didn't you know Grandma wasn't here? Where's your mom?" She didn't mention anything about his dad. She figured that Jasper was probably too little to understand that his dad had left, and maybe he didn't even know.

Actually, Terry didn't even know the latest. Why was Isadora here? Had she moved in? And where was she?

"I didn't see Isadora's car outside?"

"She's not here. I think she's at my house, and I'll tell you all about it after we get these dudes quiet," Amy said, laughing a little, but the serious sadness in her eyes made Terry feel like she was about to hear something that she definitely didn't want to. Especially coming on the heels of Sally's death the night before.

She had been so happy that Judd had been there with her. That was the kind of thing that a person didn't want to have to face alone, and Judd had made it so that she had someone to lean on, someone to draw strength from. She was sure that was what the Lord intended when He had decided it would be good for a man and woman to pair up. Their strengths complemented each other and overshadowed their weaknesses.

A human was also just programmed to grieve with someone, she thought.

She worked with Amy to change the boys, to feed Jasper some of the food that was in the refrigerator. There was baby food in the diaper bag for Landon, and then they were able to put them both down to sleep. Their mom had a room that the boys shared when they stayed over, or when any grandchildren did, with two single beds and two cribs.

It didn't leave much room for anything else in the room, but there was plenty of room for grandkids to take naps or spend the night.

Terry knew that not everyone was as blessed as they were to have a fantastic mother who enjoyed having her grandkids as much as she could. And whose life pretty much revolved around them.

They finally got Jasper to sleep, and they stood side by side, looking at Jasper, his little hand tucked up underneath his chin, his eyes closed and relaxed. And Landon, who lay on his back, his arms thrown out, his mouth open, snoring softly.

She couldn't help giving a tender smile at the innocence of the little boys.

And then her stomach tied in knots as she thought about the life that was ahead of them, and they had no idea. Likely being shuffled from home to home and never having a solid, stable environment in which to live. Where Mom and Dad fought, and Dad had girlfriends using a revolving door.

She closed her eyes and prayed that that wouldn't be their fate.

"I think they're good," Amy said, tugging on her arm.

She opened her eyes and followed her sister out the door.

Amy closed the door softly, and they went into the kitchen, with Amy putting coffee on, and Terry grabbing creamer and sugar and putting it on the bar.

"Would you rather sit at the dining room table?" she said as she set the stuff down on the counter.

"No. This is just as comfortable to me, unless you do."

"No. But I'm dying of curiosity as to what's happening with Isadora."

"I guess Clyde came back yesterday, and they decided they were going to work it out and she forgave him and it was a big thing, and then he must have been talking to his girlfriend overnight, because this morning, she woke up to him packing a suitcase and telling her he was gone for good." Amy sighed, a sound that came from her very soul. And it made Terry's heart ache in a way that she didn't realize was possible.

"He is such a jerk."

"That's what I said."

They were both quiet for a bit, remembering how their mother had tried to talk Isadora out of being with him, how she begged and pleaded, and how Isadora had said their mother was being terrible and mean and was just standing in her way and didn't know what she was talking about, and even when Isadora admitted that her mother was probably right, that she shouldn't have anything to do with an unsaved man, she admitted that she was emotionally involved and just couldn't pry herself away.

It had been terrible to see, and even though Terry and Amy both had tried to talk to Isadora, she was determined that she didn't want to hurt Clyde, and break up with him, and cause him any pain. That she was the one who had instigated the relationship, and with a dramatic flourish, she insisted that she couldn't hurt him now.

And so, it had hurt her later, along with their three children, the two that were here and the one that wasn't born yet.

"I bet she wishes she could go back and do things a little differently," Terry said, although she would never say that to Isadora. What was done was done.

"I thought the same thing over and over. She's made her bed, and I suppose like the saying goes, now she gets to lie in it. It's unfortunate that this is what it takes, because now the pain isn't just Clyde, it's Landon and Jasper and the baby that's not even born. She won't even know her dad."

"Is it a girl?"

"I'm pretty sure that's what I heard. But it's been such an eventful fall."

They were quiet for a bit, until the coffee was ready, so Terry poured them each a cup and then set them down on the counter before walking around and sitting on her stool.

"Isadora could be the poster child for teens not listening to their parents and living to regret it."

"I'm not even sure she was a teen. I'm pretty sure she was twenty-one or twenty-two. Old enough to know better," Amy said sadly.

"Yeah. I've forgotten, but you're right. Mom trusted her, and instead of doing right, she just... I think she just added him on social media or something to begin with."

"Yeah. I remember telling her that I didn't think it was a very good idea for her to be chatting with an unsaved man, and she assured me that she had it all under control, and everything would be fine, and then in the next breath, she told me not to tell Mom."

"Isn't that the way it goes? When you're doing wrong, you hide it. Nothing has changed since the Garden of Eden, when Adam and Eve sinned, and then they hid from God. Humans are so dumb."

They laughed together, and then each of them stared into their coffee cups.

"So Isadora went to your house?"

"I think so. I told her she could. It's never locked, and she just wanted someplace where she could curl up and I think just deal with the pain, you know? Like when you get hurt really bad, you just need a minute to sit there and kind of let the pain die down to some kind of throb that you can stand before you start taking care of things."

"Yeah. I totally get what you're saying," Terry said, shrugging, because there really wasn't anything they could do to help the pain that Isadora was feeling, although both of them wished they could.

Eventually, Terry, her finger running over the handle of her coffee mug, said, "I actually wanted to talk to you about... Well, I know this isn't the best timing, but I wanted some advice."

"All right," Amy said.

"Judd and I are...together."

"No way!" Amy said, jumping out of her seat and throwing her arms around Terry. "That is awesome. You would not believe the big conspiracy that the entire town has been in to try to get you two together."

"Conspiracy?" Terry said, her brows drawing down.

"I'll have to tell you later, but I'm just so excited for you." She paused. "With Gilbert losing his wife and Isadora leaving her husband, it's great that you guys have some great news."

"Yeah, I just didn't know whether we should tell everyone or not? I mean, should we wait?"

"Well, maybe my news will help you decide," Amy said slowly.

Terry's heart skipped a beat.

"Good news or bad news?" she asked, holding her breath while she waited for the answer. She wasn't sure she could take any more bad news.

"Good news, I'm pretty sure," Amy said, unable to contain her smile. "Okay, but I have to start at the beginning. Do you have time?"

"I do. Judd is making some deliveries and doing some other things, and I have as much time as I need."

"Right. So, goodness, it feels like a year ago, but just last month, Jones's aunt passed away. It was the one who wasn't talking to his parents. They got into a big fight back when Jones was around ten."

"I remember a little bit about that. Wasn't she wealthy?"

"She was. Very wealthy, and she left ten million dollars to Jones."

"You are kidding," Terry said. "Unbelievable." It was her turn to smile and put her hand on her sister's forearm. "That is so great for Jones. I know he really wants to get his vet school bills paid off, and that will more than do it."

"Right? Except, there's a catch," Amy said, looking a little unsure and giving her a sideways glance.

"And the catch is?" Hopefully it wasn't that he had to kill somebody or something. That would be straight out of a horror movie.

"The catch is that he has to be married."

"Oh my goodness. Well, you're the obvious choice."

Amy looked like she'd just had all the wind taken out of her sails. "Well then, you just jumped to the next thing I was going to tell you because we couldn't think of anyone. No one was good enough, and that's what everyone kept saying, that I was the obvious choice, and we had never really considered that, except now that we have, we decided...we're really getting married," Amy said, lifting up her hand like *what do you do*.

"Oh my goodness! Congratulations! That is awesome!" Terry was super thrilled, and it was even better because Amy was getting married at the same time she was. She couldn't help but think God had worked it out with such perfect timing.

"And so that brings me to my problem," Amy said, and Terry sobered right away. She'd forgotten there even was a problem.

"Yeah. So, the catch was he had to be married, and he had to do it within a month of her death. That's...Friday. We have to be married by Friday in order for him to get the ten million dollars. We decided that we wanted to get married whether we get the money or not. But if there's no money, we might take it slower? You know, we haven't really thought about being boyfriend and girlfriend and more, and so I think it would take us a little bit of time to get used to that, but we can hurry it up for the money. Except..."

"Sure, except, Sally passing away, the three kids don't have a mom, being so close to Christmas, now Isadora having her husband walk out, and yeah."

"Plus you. I don't want to steal your thunder. I don't want to step in and keep you from getting the attention you deserve with your engagement with Judd. I mean, this is only going to happen once in your lifetime. You want to make it special."

"Right? I do want it to be special, but I'm not worried about you stealing my thunder. I don't need any thunder," she said, trying to be emphatic about it. She didn't want her sister to not have money, not be able to do what she needed to do, just because she was concerned about Terry.

"Make me the least of your worries, okay?" she said easily. "This is not something that you even need to give two thoughts about. We can have a double wedding if you want, although I don't know what kind of wedding you're thinking about. And I don't know how Judd feels about that. I think we just wanted something small, something with just the family," she said.

"Same for us, although I'm guessing that we'll invite Jones's parents. They probably won't come, although they might? I don't know. They went to his graduation. Both college and vet school, and high school, so maybe weddings and graduations are things they attend."

Amy didn't have to say anything more. Terry had been there; she'd seen how disinterested Jones's parents had been. It was similar to Judd's parents, except Judd's parents had money. And they still weren't interested in their son.

"What is it with parents not really caring about their children? I don't understand that?"

"Me either, but our society isn't very supportive, either of children or parents having great bonds. Like it seems like it's always trying to rip the children away from the parents, send them to school, make school days longer, make school years longer, keep them there longer, get them into sports and other activities that take them away from their parents, send them to summer camps, and like you just don't see families doing things together like they used to. And then of course, both parents have to have jobs, especially moms, and she's not there to be the glue that keeps the family together, you know?"

"So just a lot of factors that seem to come together to make it so that what used to be something that was a no-brainer becomes... something that is almost nonexistent, a nuclear family that stays together for a lifetime."

"Yeah. Used to be that they had a farm, and the kids grew up and worked on the farm. It doesn't even happen that way anymore."

"So sad."

Their voices trailed off, but then Terry didn't want them to sit around and be sad about stuff they couldn't do anything about. "So there are as many good things going on as there are bad things! I wonder if it would be too terrible to try to focus on the good?"

"Good for you and me, but I don't want to not be respectful of Gilbert's grief or Isadora's pain, and I want to be cognizant that their children are suffering."

"That's so true," Terry said, knowing Amy was right. As much as she was a solid, focus on the positive kind of person, she didn't want to just ramrod over other people's trials and tribulations.

"So I don't know what to do. I mean you don't have a choice. You have to get married."

"That's just it, we don't. I mean, we can, and we'll get ten million dollars if we do, but is the ten million dollars worth being tone deaf to the pain of my family? And there is a funeral on Friday, do we want to have a wedding on Thursday?"

"What day did you have to be married by?"

"Friday."

"Have you looked it up and are one-hundred-percent sure?"

"It's been busy since then. Jones got called out, we've been helping with the children, and today is just as busy as every other day. We just found out Friday. Oh goodness, that was yesterday."

"Well."

"I know. A lot has happened. And I know it's been kind of fast, but Jones and I have been friends forever—"

"You don't have to explain to me. Judd and I haven't been together very long at all, and we haven't been good friends, we just... bonded quickly, I think. And I was able to see him in a light that I never have before. He's...everything I've ever wanted in a man."

"I'm so happy to hear it. And I'm thrilled I don't have to apologize to you or make excuses. You understand, and that's a relief. Because I did wonder what our small town is going to say if Jones and I get married that fast."

"They're going to think you're pregnant," Terry said, and they both laughed.

"And they're going to think you're pregnant too," Amy said, which caused them to laugh again.

It wasn't funny, but they weren't laughing at the sin, they were laughing at the idea that that seemed to be where everyone's minds went if someone didn't plan their wedding and make it into a big show. The idea that people wouldn't want that was almost inconceivable.

"What do you think about having it together?" Terry asked finally.

"I'd love to, and I think Jones would be fine with that if Judd is okay with it and you guys both are okay with his parents coming. Also, we're going to have trouble trying to figure out a time."

"We need to get our license. And figure out what the rules are for Virginia."

"You have to fill out an application and get a license, but once you have a license, you have sixty days to use it, and you can use it any time, even immediately."

"There is no waiting period?"

"No. None."

Terry figured that this was probably something she should talk to Judd about face-to-face, but she pulled out her phone. "I'm going to send a text and see what he says."

"All right. I can text Jones as well, but he's got three kids with him, and I might not hear anything for a while."

"That's fine. It's not an emergency that we do it quickly, and we have all day tomorrow to think about it as well."

"I figured that I would announce it to the family tomorrow at lunch. You might hear that story again, but waiting until we're all together will keep me from having to tell it a million times. I just didn't want to be insensitive to Gilbert and now Isadora."

"Isadora might not even be joining us for lunch. I saw some of my friends deal with heartbreak while I was in school, and it's not a pain that goes away quickly. It takes a long time, sometimes years until you truly don't feel anything, and even then, sometimes the bitterness and anger linger."

"Yeah. People don't understand how important it is to pick the right person to begin with."

"Not only that, but do you think there are more people who are cheating now than there used to be?"

"I don't know. It seems like it's something that people have always struggled with. Maybe there might be more women now than there used to be," Amy said softly, as though she were thinking about it.

Terry had wondered if their generation was just sinking deeper into sin, or if it was truly something that had always been a problem.

"I just feel like there's really no oversight anymore. Used to be, people were in the church, and if someone did something wrong, you had everyone looking at them going hey, don't do that wrong. But now, there isn't anyone telling them that it's wrong anymore. You know? We're all just kind of like la de da, we just don't care what you do, la de da." She knew she sounded ridiculous, but she couldn't overstate how blasé people were toward sin. And she felt like no one was holding anyone to account, and so anyone could get away with whatever they wanted to.

"You know, that's a good point. We're all about loving people and making them feel welcome and not offending them, but if they were afraid of being a social outcast, they would probably be more careful about what they did."

"I know. Our society talks about breaking down walls and crashing through old beliefs, but those walls and those old beliefs were the things that kept us safe from sin a lot of times. We knew what the consequences would be. Not just the consequences that we'll experience when God judges our sin, but the consequences of having the whole world know our sin. We'd be embarrassed, perhaps lose our jobs, be put out of society, and live a life of struggle. It was that fear that helped a lot of people decide to do right."

"But I wonder if it's better if we decide to do right on our own?

Without all of those social constraints. No one's going to excommunicate you from the church if you have an affair. No one's going to fire you if you're cheating on your husband. Even if the whole office knows it. It's just an acceptance attitude, something everybody knows. And so, if you know that there aren't going to be any social or societal repercussions, and you choose to do right anyway, doesn't that show a deeper, firmer commitment to the Lord and a higher amount of character?"

"I think you're right. But a lot of people don't have that kind of character. And I don't know what to do about it."

"Maybe it's taught when we're kids, or maybe it's the attitude of a conservative society as a whole, but trying to recreate it is kind of like trying to put the cat back in the bag. It just doesn't happen."

"No. I think you're right. But I do also think it points to the decline of our society. When there are no longer social norms to keep people's unbridled passions in check and they feel like they can do whatever they want to, that's when society starts to crumble."

"Because the family isn't stable, and that's the building block of a strong, productive society. It's been ripped apart, redefined, and that's where it starts. No moms in the home, marriages breaking up, and children being raised in an environment of instability and chaos, and we're being told that that's normal."

They were both quiet, and maybe Amy was thinking it too, but Terry was thinking about how blessed they were to have a mom and a dad who stayed together, a mom who had planned and struggled to create a haven for her children, to raise them in a home where there was love and support and stability.

It wasn't a childhood that anyone was guaranteed to have, and they had been blessed.

"Wow. We've been all over the map. Grief, breakups, surprise marriages, million-dollar inheritances, now we're solving the world's problems. This has been quite a conversation." Terry laughed and finished off the rest of her coffee.

"We haven't talked in a long time. That's probably it. Although, now that you're back, I really hope that we see you a lot more."

"I hope you do too."

Terry got up and took their cups to the sink, rinsing them out and putting them in the dishwasher.

As she did that, her phone buzzed.

> I'm fine with a double wedding. Monday, Tuesday, any day. I just want to marry you.

She read Judd's text message and smiled. "This is from Judd. He's fine getting married together, and he's fine whenever we schedule it."

"All right. I still haven't heard back from Jones, but I know that he's got his hands full with visiting and taking care of the kids. Even though they were really good help today."

"It smells like cookies in here. Is this where you made them?"

"Yep. Thankfully, Lucas was a huge help, and of course Jones was up to his elbows in everything, and I was able to get the mess cleaned up before they even left. You should have seen them, the cookies look so cute and Christmasy. They decorated most of them themselves."

"I'm glad that you were able to do something with them to try to get their mind off of losing their mom. I think a lot of times when something like this happens, families kind of sit around and just do nothing, waiting for the funeral or something. I don't know."

"We might do that later, when Mom and Gilbert get back. Although, the kids have riding therapy at two. So, hopefully there won't be much moping. But I do think it's good for them to hear different ways of coping, so they can find something that they can tell themselves."

"Yeah. To shape the way they think, and to frame it in a way that helps them get through it."

"Exactly. So maybe that's the point of everyone sitting around, because it does feel like a lot of times that's what happens. People just kind of congregate and hang out."

Terry walked back from the sink. "I know that Jones has to go to his clinic on Monday, and I have to go to mine, so Monday is probably going to be the day where you are going to need to be here as much as you can. If you need me to take over anything today or tomorrow, I can," she said, putting her hand over the top of Amy's.

"Let's see what happens when Mom and Gilbert get back. We can take it from there."

Chapter Fourteen

Jones pulled up at the horse riding stable where the kids had been going for horse riding therapy since Sally had gotten sick.

They loved the place and piled out of the car almost before he came to a stop.

"Well, I guess this is going to be one of those times we're running to catch up to them." He laughed as Amy and he got out of the car and hurried up to the children.

Summer Lubbock, who owned and operated the ranch, and did the therapy sessions, was waiting for the kids.

"You all are right on time, as you always are," she said, smiling as they came to her and then looking over their heads at Amy and Jones.

She could tell by the looks on their faces that things had not gone well, and she told the kids that they could pet the goats in the pen that was right in front while she walked over to talk to them.

This was not unusual. Often they spoke with Summer before she worked with the kids so she had an idea what was going on in their lives.

"What happened?" she asked without even greeting them.

"Sally passed away last night," Amy said, her voice pitched low, even as she watched for any indication in the children that they could hear them.

They were all looking at the goats that were heavy with the babies that would be born in the spring.

"No. That's terrible," she said, and then she said, "Is Gilbert okay?"

Amy kind of thought that Summer would have been good for Gilbert. They had known each other in high school, and Summer had a bit of a crush on him, she thought. But nothing ever came of it, of course, and now, Summer was most likely asking out of concern.

"He seemed okay last night and this morning, and we saw him for half an hour or so after he and Mom got home from making the funeral arrangements. It's going to be Friday," she said, just in case Summer wanted to go.

"Thanks for letting me know. I have enough time that I can rearrange my schedule. Is it in the afternoon?"

"Five in the evening. The viewing is before that for two hours. He didn't want to do a viewing, but being how young she was, the funeral director recommended it, saying that there would be a lot of people who would want to see her. I guess I can understand that. Also, it's going to be at our church, not the funeral home."

"All right. Thanks for the info, I'll pass it along to anyone who asks and plan to be there myself. How are the kids doing?" she asked, turning around to look at them. Lucas stood by himself, with his hands in his pockets, staring at the goats but not as into it as the two younger ones.

"It seems to hit them in waves. Sometimes they're doing fine, then Marissa especially will start crying for no reason. Robert will say, 'why can't my mom come home?'"

Amy nodded at Jones's description. Then she added, "And then other times you think from the way he's acting that he didn't even know that he had a mom. It's just hard."

"Lucas kinda has withdrawn in himself, although Judd has been working some to get him to do some things."

"I think that's the best thing to do," Summer said as she glanced at Jones. "I think Lucas is probably at the hardest age. The other two will take it hard and fast, and then I think they'll bounce back, at least outwardly, while he'll just slowly chew on it. I could be wrong," she said, glancing back over at the kids.

"Yeah. Well, we'll just keep doing what we can," Amy said, glad for Jones's comforting strength beside her.

"All right. I'm ready to get started, thanks for the info," she said, and she moved off, her cowboy boots bringing up little puffs of dust on the ground as she walked. Her arms seemed to move stiffly at her sides, probably because of the sadness and pain she felt for the children.

"She's so good with them," Jones said as she bent down to talk to the children, and all of their faces turned up to her, smiling and eager.

They went into the barn together, where Amy knew that she would have horses saddled and waiting. Her helpers would help the children get on, and then they'd go out into the arena.

Jones and she moved over to the fence. It was chilly, and she held out her hands. "Gloves," she said, showing him so he could see and be proud of her for wearing them.

"I don't recognize those. I bet your sister Terry grabbed you as you were walking out the door and probably made you put them on."

"I'm still wearing them," she said, amazed at how well he knew her, knew her family, knew everything about her. She loved it, loved that he wasn't just interested, or casually knowledgeable about what was going on her life, but knew every detail.

"How did things go with visitation?" she asked.

"It went well. Robert had one meltdown, thankfully as we were walking back to the car, and I think it was because the little kid's mom had hugged him and told him how cute his cookie was, and it made Robert think about his own mom? I'm not sure. Lucas didn't have a whole lot to say, and Marissa cried occasionally, but never loud."

"Yeah. Those loud cries are kind of hard." For everyone, including Marissa.

"It seems like it went okay, although... I don't know if we're doing the right thing."

"What else can we do? Keep them all in the house, and make them sit around and think about it?"

"Yeah. I guess put that way, I'd definitely rather be out doing something, and they seem happy now." Which was true, as all three of the kids came out riding on horses, while Summer was on her own horse, giving instructions.

Summer had a lot of rescue horses, although many of her rescues were Gypsy Vanner mares, who were too old to have babies or hadn't been trained when they were younger. She'd work with them, and the thing about her horses was they were beautiful, so the kids loved riding them. They also had a lot of hair in their manes and tails, and the kids enjoyed brushing and grooming them as well.

A lot of times, Summer started with that, but as their mother had gotten progressively worse, they spent more time riding.

"This always helps the kids. I know when they come home from this, it always seems to soothe their souls somehow."

"You and I both know there's something about animals that calls to an inner part of us that is hard to ignore. I couldn't even explain it if I tried."

"Yeah. Animals do seem like they don't judge us, you know? They love us unconditionally, no matter what. Of course, they expect us to feed them, but that's not really something you think about when you're a kid."

"And occasionally they bite or scratch, but if you can explain it as them being scared or hurt, then you can typically let it go and love them for just what they are."

They fell into silence and watched the happy smiles of the children as they rode the horses around the ring, their chests jutting out as Summer gave them a compliment or their faces moving in concentration as she gave them a suggestion to implement.

She seemed to know just when they could handle some helpful hints and just when they needed to be encouraged.

"It probably wouldn't hurt Gilbert to have some therapy with her. I know she does adults too. Or maybe he could just ride with his kids," Amy said thoughtfully.

"Are you matchmaking, or are you trying to help your brother?"

"Isn't that one and the same?" she asked, looking up at him. Again, not amazed, but enjoying the fact that he knew her so well.

"I don't know. You tell me."

"Isn't every human happier when they have someone beside them?"

"I don't know about that. I think some people are just naturally loners."

She thought about that. That seemed to be Roland, her brother. But he was more of an introvert. And Wilson was like that as well.

"Do you think men are more like that than women?" she asked.

"No. I think there are plenty of women who enjoy being alone."

"I still think even if you're an introvert, you still want to be married. You still want to have that mate beside you, someone who is with you when things go wrong and who celebrates with you when things go right."

He put his hands on the fence and leaned on it while he didn't take his eyes off the kids. "I think you're probably right. Although I still think there are a few exceptions to the rule, introverts and extroverts both want to have that someone who loves them no matter what."

"I agree. Although, come to think of it, maybe we do want that and it's built into us, but we don't realize that that's God, you know? He loves us no matter what."

"That's deep. But I agree," Jones said, sounding kind of surprised.

She was going to give him a hard time for not thinking that she could think deeply, but she knew better, and she wanted to talk about something else.

"Are you sure you're okay with us doing the wedding with Terry and Judd?"

"Yeah. I said I was."

"I wanted to make sure that you weren't just saying it because you knew that that would be something that would be kinda special for me."

"No. That's fine. Although, I haven't told my parents yet."

"Maybe after this, we can take a drive down?" she suggested, knowing that he might not want to. Visiting his parents could be an exercise in feeling unloved and unwanted.

He'd mostly gotten over that through the years. It seemed the closer he got to her family, the more the betrayal of his family didn't bother him.

"I think that's a good idea," he said, not really sounding like it was, more like sounding like he knew they had to.

"When are we going to announce it to your family?" he asked, probably thinking that maybe her family deserved to know before his.

"We'll probably be getting together with everyone this evening, and Terry and Judd will probably tell everyone they're getting married. I need to finalize that with Terry, but I figure that you and I could tell everyone tomorrow. That's if Terry doesn't tell anyone this evening. Because I want them to hear it from us."

"We'll be there this evening, so if the subject comes up, we can talk about it, but I agree, Terry and Judd should have their day, and you and I get tomorrow."

"Yeah. Neither one of us are big divas. I know for sure that I don't really care about having my own day or whatever, but I do care about my family knowing and about me telling them. I don't think I'm keeping information from them. But I also want to be respectful of Gilbert."

"Yeah. He had a pretty big loss, and it might be a big stretch to ask him and Isadora to be happy for both of you."

She realized she hadn't told him about Isadora, so she filled him in quickly.

He flattened his lips and shook his head. "I remember her fighting with your mom and your mom watching as she walked out of the house, determined to do things her own way, and your mom just collapsing in a chair and crying, and I thought at first that she was upset because Isadora wouldn't listen and she was being disobedient, but I think she was crying because she could see all of this coming."

"Yeah. I know that's why. And I know Isadora knows that she should have listened, I think she probably knew it a long time ago, and has been regretting it ever since."

"She will regret it the rest of her life."

"But we can't fix that, you know? I mean, we can't go back and get her to listen. At the time, there just wasn't anything you could say that would change her mind, and it makes me wonder if I'm ever like that?"

He grinned at her. "Sometimes you do kinda get the bit in your mouth and go running off thinking that you've got the next new greatest idea, and nothing anybody says is going to convince you that you're wrong."

"You could convince me," she said, and she really felt confident about that, although she was kinda scared that she would become like Isadora and not listen to the people who were trying to help her, but instead go to her friends who would tell her what she wanted to hear.

Jones was a friend.

"You know, the story about Rehoboam in the Bible. Solomon's son. And how when he took over from Solomon and he asked the elders what he should do, and then he asked his friends, and he ended up taking his friends' advice. He was foolish."

"Hmm. I don't even know if Isadora had heard that, and been

able to apply it to herself, if she would have been able to make herself do right. She admitted that she knew that she was not making a wise decision, but she wanted to do it anyway."

"You know what, I think there are a lot of people like that. Probably more than what we know. People who know that they're sinning, and they do it anyway."

"Yeah. I think it goes back to what Terry and I were talking about earlier today. It didn't have anything to do with all the things that were going on. Maybe we just needed to distract ourselves, but we talked about how in society today, there aren't any limitations. It used to be, you did something wrong, and people gathered round and told you about it. You felt ostracized, judged, ridiculed, and you might be fired from your job, lose friends, be excommunicated from the church. It kept people from doing wrong, and now, there's nothing like that. In fact, if anyone does anything like that, they're the ones who are ostracized because they're not tolerant or whatever. There are no boundaries, no walls, we've broken those down, and people act proud about it, but I guess I don't see it as a good thing."

"Not unless you're the one who's done wrong and you want someone to hold your hand and tell you that it's okay, you're still wonderful and fine."

"Yeah. Like we're doing with Isadora. I love her, and I don't think I could ostracize her in any way, but..."

"Maybe back when she had made those bad decisions. But she'd just have found new friends and gotten other people to tell her what she wanted to hear."

"Yeah." She paused. "You know with all this going on, I'm not sure that Gilbert has even thought about Christmas gifts for his kids." The idea just came to her. It was less than two weeks before Christmas, and he didn't have a whole lot of time.

"I heard that someone has that under control," Jones said slowly.

"Oh, you have?" Amy asked, looking at her friend with new eyes. What did he know that she didn't?

"Yeah. I heard from a little bird that the Secret Saint was going to be taking care of them."

"Is that so?" Amy said, suspicion narrowing her eyes. "Does that mean you know who the Secret Saint is?"

"No," Jones said slowly. "But I know someone who knows."

"Well, that's more than a lot of people know, including Terry, because she's been asking in her column almost every day who the Secret Saint could possibly be and begging anyone who has any information to let her know." Her sister Terry was in charge of the social media posts for the Secret Saint and the town of Mistletoe Meadows.

"Yeah." Jones didn't say anything more, and Amy got the feeling that he knew more than he was talking about, but she also knew that there was a huge amount of secrecy involving the Secret Saint. She should honor that and not try to get Jones to tell her everything he knew.

"All right. I'm not going to bug you about it, as long as you don't tell anyone else any information. Because if you tell other people things you won't tell me, you know I'm going to be really mad about that."

"You're so cute when you're mad," Jones said, ignoring everything she said.

"Jones Quebedeau. I mean it."

He put his arm around her and pushed her head against his chest, ruffling her hair at the same time. "You might not know this, but I wouldn't dream of telling someone else stuff that I don't tell you. You're the first one to hear everything that's going on in my life. I don't even have a sister to sit around chatting with and then text you about what we decided we want to do."

"You said you didn't mind!" she said, her words muffled by his chest, before she was able to pull herself away and look up into his smiling face.

"And I don't. And I won't tell anyone anything that I don't tell you first, or I'll at least text you immediately and tell you what I said. Deal?"

She appreciated that he took it seriously that she really did want to know who the Secret Saint was, but she didn't want to make him tell her and break a confidence or get in trouble in any way.

"I talked to Wilson."

"Are you serious? First of all, you told me you weren't going to tell me, then you told me. That's my brother?" Wilson was the Secret Saint?

"Yeah. But he's not the actual Secret Saint. Wilson just said that the Secret Saint had contacted him and wanted to know if you could find out what exactly Gilbert's kids might like for Christmas, since he was assuming that Gilbert was going to have trouble getting anything. So he asked if I could find out and then let him know so he could let the Secret Saint know."

"Like playing telephone where all the information is scrambled up by the time it goes through too many people?"

"Yeah?"

"This feels like that. Marissa is going to ask for a doll, and she's going to end up getting a truck or something."

"Do they even make Tonka trucks anymore?"

"You are missing the point." She rolled her eyes.

"No. I understand. But I know that I am not the best person to come up with a list of things for the kids, and I'm pretty sure that Wilson figured that I would talk to you about it. I think he was hoping that I wouldn't tell you who he was, but you know better."

"Yeah. I'd like to give him a piece of my mind, except... I won't, because I don't want him to know you told me."

"I appreciate it, although don't lie. For goodness' sake."

"I won't."

The kids had turned their horses and were headed into the barn. There were still twenty minutes left of the session, and Amy figured that they'd be brushing them. Those beautiful long manes and tails could provide a lot of therapy.

"You want to go in and watch them?" Jones asked as he dropped his foot from the bottom rail where he had rested it and moved his forearms off the top, straightening out.

"Yeah. Then we're going to your parents?"

"Yeah. I guess we'll let them know what we're doing. Although something tells me that they're not going to care."

Chapter Fifteen

Jones gripped the wheel as they pulled into a spot directly in front of his parents' house along the street.

If Mistletoe Meadows had a bad side of town, this would be it.

It hadn't been terrible growing up, and that thought hadn't really occurred to him until he had grown up and moved out of the house.

Still, there was no yard to speak of. And the houses on either side were right next door. He could reach out his window and touch hands with the person who lived beside him.

Sometimes he'd lie in bed and wonder how in the world they'd made the houses. How had they gotten them so close? How did they manage to put them up without even enough room for scaffolding on the outside?

Regardless, they'd done it, and they built a house that had been able to stand for his entire lifetime so far, anyway.

At least his parents had stayed together. A lot of kids had gone through divorces or been raised by single parents. Shuffled back and forth. It had been hard for them. Although, some of them acted like it was normal. For them, it was. It wasn't the way it was supposed to be.

"Are you okay?" Amy asked as she got out of her car and shut the door while he walked around.

"I'm fine. It's never pleasant, no matter how much I've accomplished, it never feels like it's enough, or maybe it feels like it's too much. I don't know. I just know they're not going to care, and I don't know why I do sometimes."

He hated that he still wanted his parents' approval, even though they never really seemed interested in him. He'd have thought he'd learned by now, but it seemed like it was something that was hardwired into kids to want their parents' love and approval.

"Because you love them. Love them, and no matter how they treat you, you've always been kind to them and good to them. Far better than they deserve," she said, coming along beside him and, after a pause, tentatively slipping her hand into his.

That made him smile. He liked this new dimension to their relationship. He was sure about the way it was going, sure they were doing the right thing, but it was still new and a little tentative, on both of their parts. He thought they were probably going to be rushing things a bit by getting married so soon, but nothing said that they had to change anything about the relationship before they were ready. They would just have a marriage certificate between them. He intended to talk to Amy about that too. Not that he minded kissing her, because he didn't, and he thought about it pretty much all the time now, but even though he was thinking about it, it didn't mean that he was ready to shift gears and take off in an entirely new direction. He felt like he just wanted to ease into it. And he was pretty sure that was how Amy felt too.

They walked up the porch together, her fingers tight around his, whether she was scared, nervous, or trying to give him strength, he wasn't quite sure. Maybe it was a combination of all of it.

He was sure his parents were home; their car was out front. They shared one, since his mom was able to walk to work at the local dollar store just down the street. That was when she decided to work. She'd been hired and fired from there at least four different times, and in the meantime, she worked as a bartender, at a drugstore, and as a part-time babysitter, which kind of scared him. Not that she had ever abused him, but her apathy toward children didn't tend to make him think that she would make the best babysitter. Of course, she'd raised him and he hadn't died, so maybe he was judging her too harshly.

"You ready?" he asked, feeling like he'd already said that in the car, but maybe he just needed one more second.

"Let's do this thing," she said, giving him a smile that projected confidence, and he appreciated that about her.

He opened the door, calling out, "Mom! Dad! It's Jones," as they walked in, and he carefully shut the door behind them.

The TV blasted, and the house smelled faintly of cigarette smoke, although he couldn't remember his parents ever smoking. It had smelled like that for as long as he could remember. Perhaps from the people who lived there before. The carpet was the same that he'd grown up with, and maybe that was where the scent came from. His mom wasn't a terrible housekeeper, although she didn't do any more than was strictly necessary.

"Mom? Dad?" He took a step in the entryway and leaned in, looking in the living room. There were steps up to his right and a hall that went back to the kitchen. It was a bigger house than the apartment he lived in right now over the garage of his clinic, but every time he walked in, it seemed smaller, even though there were no children here since he'd grown up and moved out.

They kept their eyes on the TV set until he said one more time, maybe a little bit louder, "Mom? Dad?"

"Jones? And that's Amy," his mom said, peeling her eyes away from the TV, a little bit of interest lighting her eyes. He wasn't sure if his dad's eyes flicked to him or not.

"Duffy. Look away from the TV. Jones is here."

His dad grunted, but he did what his wife asked.

"Is there something going on?" she asked, and he felt a little bit bad. Did he really visit that seldom?

"Amy and I are going to get married this week." There. He got the news out, and he noted that his dad didn't seem the slightest bit surprised, and while his mom's eyes might have flickered, she nodded.

"Well, that's great. Congratulations." She nodded again and didn't seem to know what else to say.

His dad had gone back to staring at the TV, despite the fact that the sound was turned down.

"So yeah, if you guys want to come to the wedding, you can."

"Oh? When is it?" his mom said, lifting a shoulder. "I'll have to check my schedule at the dollar store," she said, without giving him a chance to answer.

"We were thinking about doing it Monday afternoon. Around six, after Jones gets off work."

"Oh. Okay. Yeah, usually I work Mondays, but yeah, I'll try to make it if I can. Duffy?" She looked at her husband.

He grunted.

"Can you make Jones's wedding?"

"I don't know. If you go, I'll probably go too."

This whole conversation was so awkward. His parents seemed to care, but not too much. Or something, he wasn't even sure. He was embarrassed. He knew that when Amy told her mom, she'd practically flip out and want to start taking control of all the decorations and everything, but she'd back off when Amy asked her to, and the whole family would be happy and begging them to take a little bit longer so everyone could make plans and help out, but they'd understand why they didn't want to and... His parents just made it so that he wasn't even sure he wanted to go on and tell them about the money and about sharing the day with Amy's sister. Amy would let him say whatever he wanted to. And if he decided not to tell them some things, she wasn't going to loudly remind him or tell them herself. She would trust his judgment. Even if she thought he should say more than what he was.

He appreciated that about her.

"I'll check my schedule and see what we can do. Six o'clock should be fine, if your dad gets off at three. And I might be able to trade with someone, but if I can't, I hope it's really nice," she said, nodding and smiling at Amy. "I'm sure you'll be a beautiful bride. Do you have a dress picked out?"

"No. I'll probably just wear something from my closet. It's not going to be very big."

"Oh. Okay," his mom said, seeming more surprised that Amy wasn't concerned about her dress than she was that they were getting married in a week.

There was an awkward silence as Jones tried to figure out something else to say.

"How have you guys been?"

"Good. We've been good," she said, smiling at him, then her eyes drifted to the TV. He felt like he was interrupting something. Although, with electronics now, he figured they could pause it at the very least. But from the changing light that reflected against the wall and their faces, he could tell that they had only muted it.

"Well, I guess I don't want to take up any more of your time. It looks like you're watching something interesting,"

"Oh, we are. It's this really fun talk show, and this guy's going to find out that his wife's been cheating on him and his son isn't really his. I can't wait to see what they're going to say."

"All right. Well, I'll let you get back to it then." He felt embarrassed that his parents would rather watch a talk show than talk to him. "I'll see you guys maybe Monday?"

"Maybe. We'll try to be there, honey. Nice to see you, Amy," his mom said.

Jones sighed and walked back out to the foyer, opening the door for Amy, and they both stepped out into the clean, fresh air. It always felt like having a noose release from his neck, getting out of that house.

"Stepping out of there always feels like freedom," he said softly.

"I'm sorry. Every time we talk to them, I feel so uncomfortable. Because I know they're just hurting you, and I can't do anything about it."

"There's a lot of pain in the world, and we can't do anything about a lot of it."

"I know. But that doesn't change the fact that I want to, you know?"

"Yeah. I understand," he said, knowing what she meant.

She laid her head on his shoulder for just a moment, and then they walked off the porch and to the car, with him opening the door for her and her getting in.

There probably wasn't much to do about his parents, other than keep trying, but it was hard not to get discouraged. Still, he could try not to let that happen in his own family. He was determined that that would be the case.

Chapter Sixteen

Isadora's car was still at Amy's house when they got back from visiting his parents. So, they fed the dogs and animals without going in. Amy didn't see any movement, and while she could be sleeping, she was worried about Isadora.

"I'm going to text her, just to see that everything is okay, and as long as she answers me back, I don't need to go in."

She didn't think Isadora was so upset that she would do anything drastic, but she knew that she absolutely could be wrong. She'd never had a heartbreak like that, and she couldn't use her own life's experience as a judge. Everyone's experience was different, anyway.

"All right. Go ahead. I'm going to take the grain over to the horses," Jones said as he shoveled a scoop of grain in each bucket and carried it over to where Belle's and Bob's feed containers were hooked on the fence.

Are you okay? Just let me know you're still alive and you don't need anything, and then I'm going to head to Mom's.

She hit send on her phone and tried not to fidget as she waited for an answer. They had pretty much everything done, and she realized that she should have texted before they started. That would have given Isadora time to see her text and respond.

I'm fine. You can come in if you want to. I'm curled up in your bed. This thing is comfy.

She read the text, relieved, even smiling that Isadora seemed okay. For some reason, the idea that Isadora was going to do something drastic had taken a hold of her mind, and she couldn't get rid of the thought.

Now, she knew she was okay and could tell her family that too.

She shoved her phone in her pocket, walked over to meet Jones as he dumped the feed in, and checked the water trough.

It was getting colder, although the temperatures were supposed to rise before they fell during the storm that was now forecasted to come on Tuesday.

He stopped to scratch Bob's head, and Amy went to Belle, so she wouldn't feel left out.

"Is she okay?" Jones asked, and Amy nodded.

"She's fine. She's still in bed, but I think maybe she just needs rest. She hasn't had a chance to...grieve? Is that too strong of a word? I mean after all, her marriage died. Would it follow the same pattern as an actual death?"

"I'm not too big on the patterns of grief or whatever, but I think you're right. I think it would be a grieving process. Like you said, her relationship is dead, and her dreams for the future as well."

"Yeah. Just everything that she thought has been yanked out from underneath her." They'd already talked about it, so she tried not to go into it again. Although she figured that the family would be talking about it this evening.

"I just want to thank you for...not being like Clyde," she said, looking down before looking back up and meeting his eyes as the daylight faded.

His lips quirked up a bit, but the smile didn't quite reach his eyes. Perhaps because he knew that she was complimenting him, but he was still sad about her sister. And somehow he was able to balance both of those things.

"I guess I could thank you for not being like my parents. For sharing your family and your life with me. Although, that's probably not the thing I'm most grateful for," he said as he put a casual arm around her shoulders and they walked back to the barn to put the buckets away and close the doors.

"No? What is?" she asked, curious.

"Your friendship. No one else has ever been the kind of friend to me that you have. Through everything. I mean, I know I can disagree with you, and you know I can be maddening, but you're not going to think I'm an idiot. In fact, if I disagree with you, you're gonna try as hard as you can to figure out my side. Even if we never do come to an agreement. And you know me. I don't know if you deliberately take the time to know me, or I just forced it upon you where you've had no choice, but there isn't another person in the world who knows me like you do."

"I think that's just the way friendships go, isn't it? We know each other, and we spend a lot of time together and learn things, and it's kind of natural. All friendships are like that."

"Do you have another friendship like that?" he asked.

She thought for a bit. "My sisters?" she suggested, knowing that that was partially true. "But they don't know me as well as you do. Not nearly. I guess I just appreciate you being there. You know? I don't have to ask, I don't have to wonder if you're going to show up. You always do. Even if you don't do anything, because a lot of times there's nothing to do. It's just boring, sitting with me, but you're there. Like tonight. I can't imagine anything's going to happen. We're just going to be a family sitting around, being with Gilbert. Because his wife died, and his kids need us and he needs us and we're just there."

"But that's just it. That *is* doing something. It's doing something, even if it's nothing, because you could be doing something else. You know?"

"Yeah. I guess that's what I meant. I know you could be doing something else, but you're not. You're with me. And I know as long as I need you, you'll always be there. I don't even have to think about it."

"That's the way I want to be. I don't want you to have to wonder if I'm going to be around. And you make it so that I don't have to wonder if you're going to think I'm a terrible person. I know you're not."

"You're still feeling bad about your parents, aren't you?" she said, wishing for the millionth time that there was something she could do about that. They reached the barn, and she set the buckets in, stepping back out while he closed the door.

"You know it always gets me down. Not for long, but it's just discouraging. I don't even really understand them. I mean, Mom's polite, Dad's...too drunk to talk, I guess, I don't know. Maybe they care and I just can't see it. Maybe our love languages are different or something." He kicked a foot on the stones, making a couple of dogs bark, as they walked by the pens and toward her car.

"Maybe." She couldn't explain his parents either. She had no idea what was up with them. Had never been able to understand. But the Lord had worked it out that Jones had been able to basically grow up in her family.

"I guess I don't even really care anymore. If your parents had been better, you and I might not be friends right now. Or as good of friends. You'd have spent more time with your parents, maybe they'd have had more kids? It just wouldn't have worked out nearly as well if your parents would have been different. And I'm not sad about that. I mean I'm sad for you, and I know it hurts you, but I love the way God worked it out. He took something that could have been terrible, and he gave me a best friend because of it."

"He gave me a best friend because of it, too." He paused, and then he said, "And a wife."

"Wow. That's pretty unbelievable, isn't it?"

"It's too fast. We don't have to do it—"

"No. That wasn't what I was saying. I want to do it. Not just for the money, but I would want to do it anyway. Now that we thought about it. It's just, wow."

He nodded as he reached the car, walking over to her side and opening her door.

"This is new," she said, glinting her eyes at him and smiling a bit.

"I know. I thought about it, and I don't know, it seemed like when we were just friends, I didn't really think about it, but now I think I should be treating you a little bit differently. Not changing anything, and that's why I didn't talk about it, just changing the position that you have in my life. It's always been best friend, but it's a little bit more now, you know?"

His thought warmed her to her toes. He truly had thought about it, and he had done something to show that he had thought about it. Not just thought about it and then never let her know what was going on in his head.

It meant a lot to her that he took action to go along with his words. Saying something was so easy. But doing something? That showed he truly meant it. At least to her.

Of course, he could have truly meant it without doing anything, but she loved that he wasn't the kind of man who didn't have actions to follow his words.

She could see that in Clyde back when Isadora had him around before they were married. Clyde talked a big talk, about how much he loved her and all that, but when it came down to the little things, things that someone in love might do for the person that they loved, he didn't do any of those little things. It wasn't glaringly obvious, but it definitely stopped her and made her think.

They got in the car, and he started the engine, backing out slowly and heading toward her parents' house.

"So we're going to try not to tell anyone about you and me until tomorrow, because we're leaving tonight for Terry and Judd, am I right?" he said, and she appreciated that he was trying to make sure that he was in the loop and doing the right thing.

"That's right, but if it comes out, it comes out, and we're not going to get concerned about it. Terry already said that she's okay, but that one shoe dropping at a time is probably better than two shoes dropping at once."

"All right then. Let's head to your parents' house and celebrate Terry and Judd."

Chapter Seventeen

arjorie looked around the room, happy and sad and torn.

It was almost Christmas, and usually this was a time to celebrate, but with Gilbert, who sat in a recliner with Marissa on his lap while Robert played at his feet and Lucas stood in a corner with his gaze fixed on the floor, losing his wife, it was hard to feel festive. And then, everything that was happening with Isadora just made it all worse.

She hadn't gotten a chance to talk to Isadora much, and she figured that Isadora was probably ashamed.

Marjorie had been pretty hard on her back when she had decided that she was going to be with Clyde. Marjorie had seen the train wreck coming from the very first second and had done what any rational parent would do—tried as hard as she could to keep her child out of danger. And from getting hurt.

Maybe she'd come on too strong. Maybe she had overwhelmed Isadora to the point where she felt like her only choice was to be with Clyde. But she didn't really think so. Isadora had told her that she knew it was wrong, but she was going to do it anyway.

She didn't think that there were any other words that could break a mother's heart faster or harder than those. All the years of teaching. All the years of raising her to do right. All the years of watching as she grew and praying that she would do the right thing, all those years, all that effort, all that time, totally wasted as Isadora put her nose in the air and determined that she was going to be with someone who was absolutely not God's will for her.

And the only reason Marjorie knew that was because the man wasn't saved. He might have been a good man, and Marjorie had told her that, but she also knew it didn't matter how good the man was. If he wasn't saved, Isadora had no business with him.

Isadora wouldn't listen. It was kind of like the people who were surrounding Noah when he was building the ark. Noah knew what was going to happen, and he tried to warn them, but they wouldn't listen. So many times, God's people wouldn't listen.

The situation with Isadora had made Marjorie take stock of her own life. Were there times when she wasn't listening?

Regardless, it was too late to do anything about it now. Clyde was gone, Isadora was a mess, and her two babies needed help.

Marjorie had told Amy to go on when she had gotten home and seen that the kids were napping. She was a little bit old to be watching five children. Although, she'd do whatever it took to help her kids out. That's just the way things went when you were a mom. At least for her.

Still, she thought Terry and Judd might have some good news for them. They had been talking and smiling at each other, and Marjorie was happy for them. Judd was a good man, and Terry deserved someone just like him.

She loved what he'd been doing with kids on Sundays, bringing them to church in his wagon.

The church had brought plenty of food in. Someone had brought a vegetable tray, and Marjorie knew that her kids loved the dill pickle dip with their vegetables, along with the ranch dip that had been provided. So, she went over to the refrigerator and checked to see if she had the ingredients. It was extremely simple, and she got the dill pickles out, intending to chop them up. She liked them in small pieces, small enough to be picked up easily when a person dipped their veggie sticks in.

The door opened, and her head came up. Wilson.

He'd gotten lost in the shuffle, and she wondered what was going on with him. They hadn't had a chat for a while, and she didn't really know what was happening in his life. She smiled though, when she saw he had brought his guitar.

Fond memories of when the kids were little and they used to sing together filled her heart and mind, and she hoped that they would sing some tonight. Singing was a balm to the soul, and she knew that even in the deepest trials, God still wanted to hear them praise Him.

Her kids had never sung anything except for praise to the Lord, and she knew those were the kinds of songs that would help them now.

"Can I give you a hand, Mom?" Terry said, coming around the counter and standing beside her.

"I'm making dill pickle dip, and you can help if you'd like. But you can just stand there and chat if you want." She smiled at her daughter. She knew Terry was so happy to be home. She wanted to be able to help, and it had killed her when she had been away so long.

"I'm glad I'm back. There are so many things happening, and I would be dying if I weren't here." She spoke as she opened the refrigerator and got out the cream cheese and sour cream.

"You know the Lord works these things out. Things were pretty smooth sailing while you were gone. Other than the debacle with Isadora, but you're here now to see the fallout from that, so that's something."

"I wonder if I'd been here if I could have gotten her to listen to me."

"Maybe. You're her oldest sister, and I know she respected you. But I think her mind was made up. Sometimes I wonder if maybe the devil gets a hold of us and we don't even realize it. Do we open our minds in some way to him so that he has a foothold there? I know we have a spiritual war going on that we can't see. But... I wouldn't hold yourself accountable, because my head says it wouldn't have made a difference."

"Thanks. I know that makes things a little bit easier for me. I just feel so terrible for her, and what can you do?"

"I know. There's nothing you can say, nothing you can do, other than sit there and listen when she wants to talk, and just hold her—"

"Watch her kids, so that she can try to come to grips with the pain."

"Yeah. I think right now she really wants him back. Even though he's cheated, and she has to hate him too." Marjorie felt bad saying that, but she thought it was true.

"Yeah. I hate him. That's for sure. If she wants him back, I'm not the person to talk to, because I would be more likely to talk about how to dissect his eyeballs or something."

"Oh goodness. I'd say that's the doctor in you coming out, but I'm afraid...it might be Mr. Hyde."

It was a joke that not a whole lot of people would get, but Terry did, and she laughed. That was one of the best things about being with family and, in particular, with her children. She'd homeschooled them all for their first eighteen years, and they had so many shared experiences, they could tell inside jokes all day long.

The door opened, and Amy and Jones came in.

"Oh, they must be done feeding the dogs," Terry said as she put the beaters in the mixer. "I'm so glad to see them here."

"Me too," Marjorie said, smiling at Amy and Jones and how they were bantering, even as they came in the door. They toned it down, out of respect for the fact that Gilbert was probably here, and they were correct.

The Christmas lights, the few that she'd gotten up, twinkled in the tree, where it sat half decorated, and still lent a sort of festivity to the place. She'd gotten the lights on with the kids, but she hadn't been able to go get the bulbs and the other decorations. There had been too much going on. Too many things happening, too much that needed her attention. Children and grandchildren that needed her, and the Christmas decorations would just have to wait. She had plenty of years with beautiful decorations, and this was not going to be one of them. And she was not going to get upset or huffy about it. Some years were good, some years weren't, and that was the way life went.

"Hey, Mom!" Amy called from where she and Jones were taking their coats and hats off and hanging them up. The kids had come running over, and Marissa had her arms around Amy's waist while Lucas was excitedly talking to Jones about something that he and Judd had done the other day. It was like the kids hadn't seen them earlier.

Amy and Jones would make such a great couple, but they never seemed to notice that, although there did seem to be something different about them tonight. Marjorie narrowed her eyes. If there was, she knew that Amy wasn't going to keep it from her. Some of her children might not talk to her as much as others, but Amy was one that always cared about how she felt and what she thought, and while Amy did not necessarily hesitate to do things, she definitely always took her mother's opinion to heart.

She had been a great child.

She scraped the pickles that she had chopped into a bowl. They didn't measure too much, usually just eyeballed things, and she decided that maybe one more would be sufficient.

Terry had the mixer started, and that muted the conversation for a bit, as Marjorie thought back to happier times, which was pretty much every other year, other than the year they had to deal with Isadora.

Roland was a bit of a wild card too, but he seemed to be coming around.

Lord, it would be nice to get some happy news tonight. Just something encouraging.

She couldn't even think of what might be encouraging. Just something so they weren't focused on grief and the funeral they would soon be attending. Gilbert probably needed that, especially.

To her surprise, the door opened just as Marjorie shut the mixer off, and Isadora slipped in.

Amy and Jones had gone over to Gilbert who was sitting in the recliner, and Marjorie didn't think that they saw Isadora come in.

"I'm going to go over and greet her," she said to Terry.

"I'm coming with," Terry said, setting the mixer down and wiping her hands on a dish towel.

They went around the counter, and both of them hugged Isadora from opposite sides as she turned from hanging up her coat.

"I'm so glad you were able to come. I was worried about you."

"I'm fine, Mom. Just...tired, sad, you know. All the things."

"I know. We're here to help you. And you're welcome to just hang out here if you want to."

"I appreciate you all watching my children," she said as she looked around the room, seeing Jasper playing on the floor and Landon in a high chair in the kitchen where Marjorie had been working.

He had Cheerios on the tray in front of him, and as she looked, he saw her and started hitting his tray and happily saying, "Mama! Mama!"

"They miss you, but they're happy when you're not here. They'd be happier with you." Marjorie hoped she was saying the right thing. She didn't want Isadora to think that her kids didn't care, but she also didn't want her to worry about them, because she would take good care of them until Isadora was able to do it herself. She understood how debilitating heartbreak could be. She had experienced it once herself. Of course, in different circumstances, but still.

"I know you don't understand—"

"I lost your dad. I know how I felt then. I just wanted to get in bed and never get out. Maybe that's not the way you feel—"

"It's exactly how I feel," Isadora said, but her eyes dropped, and then she said, "but my pain was avoidable. I didn't listen. I just wanted you to know I'm sorry."

"And I want you to know that that is water under the bridge and I don't care. It's too late to do anything about it." She didn't want Isadora to think that she wasn't going to let it go. They could talk about it if she wanted to, and sometimes Marjorie did wonder if there was something she could have done. Something that would have convinced her to not do wrong, but then again, Isadora would have missed this, and maybe this was the growing experience that she needed to understand how to become a strong Christian without her mother there pushing her in the right direction.

Although, Marjorie didn't think there was anything at all wrong with parents pushing their children to do right. As they grew older, they could learn from the pain of others, and not their own pain, if they allowed themselves to be spared from it. If they didn't, they were the warning for other people.

"Come on in. Terry and I are making dill pickle dip, and we have plenty of food."

"I'm not hungry."

"I was not hungry after Dad died either." She paused, weighing her words, and then she said, "But I wasn't pregnant."

Isadora's mouth flattened, and then she grimaced. "Good point, Mom. Thanks. You always have good advice. I just don't always listen." She tilted her head and met her mom's eyes, and Marjorie's heart just broke. There was so much pain and sadness and regret in Isadora's face that she could hardly stand it.

"God takes people's messes, and He makes beautiful things out of them. We just have to trust Him and hold on tight. And I think your repentance, your apology, your admittance that you did wrong, is the first step. God loves humility."

"I can hear you saying that as a child, and it resonates as an adult even louder." Isadora reached and gave her another hug. "I love you, Mom."

Her words made Marjorie's chest feel warm and soft, even though there was still a tight ball of pain right in the middle of it. How she had longed to hear those words back when Isadora had determined that she was not going to listen but was going to do things her own way. She had wanted so much to know that Isadora loved her and would do the right thing, and she had had to wait for years, but it had finally happened.

Thank you, Lord, for bringing my lost sheep home.

She heard a few strums of the guitar, and then Wilson began singing.

He started with "Amazing Grace," which was not Marjorie's favorite. She'd heard it at so many funerals that it brought more sadness than anything. In fact, even as she listened, her eyes filled with tears. This would be the first Christmas in more than a decade that Sally wasn't with them. They were going to have to go to her funeral and celebrate her life, then bury her, as the season of happiness and joy went on around them.

She hoped Gilbert was up for the task. She knew she was happy that she hadn't lost her husband over the holidays. That would have made it twice as difficult. And then every year after that, the holidays would have been sad and depressing. Unless she could have allowed God to show her the way to get out of that pit.

She knew He had the ability to make the holidays a happy time, but she just didn't know if she was strong enough to do what it took to make it happen.

And she wasn't sure if she would have had the willpower to do it either. It was so much easier to wallow in grief, misery and memories. As much as she didn't want to admit it.

The entire family had started singing, other than she and Terry who had gone back to the kitchen to finish up the pickle dip. Terry scraped the cream cheese mixture in, they added a couple other ingredients, and Marjorie got the vegetables out of the refrigerator and set them on the counter, in case people wanted to eat. They weren't having a sit-down meal, it was just feed yourself when you were hungry.

Isadora had gotten Landon out of his high chair, and she'd gone in and sat down on the floor beside Jasper, who seemed thrilled to have his mother and brother beside him again.

Wilson sang all the verses of "Amazing Grace," and Marjorie was again astounded at her son's memory. He knew all the words to every song in the hymnbook. At least the ones he'd sung. Somehow, he just had a knack for it. He could play the chords on the guitar to accompany them as well. He'd always been the leader when they sang, once he was old enough. And she appreciated it, since she wasn't very good.

He began another hymn, one that maybe seemed out of season, but one that spoke to her heart more than any other, probably her favorite hymn. "How Great Thou Art."

She listened to the verses, as her children sang in harmony, and then smiled as the music swelled on the chorus.

That was the song of her heart. That God was great, no matter what was going on in her life. She listened to her children singing, listened to the harmony, saw the generations sitting on the floor, and thought about her husband.

He hadn't been around much, and maybe that was for the best. Her thoughts turned next to the Lord. It was because of God that her children were sitting there, singing praises to Him in harmony, and holding their kids, supporting each other, and doing what they could to get along. God had been so very, very good to her, and no matter how their Christmas turned out, this was the best gift her children, or the Lord, could give her.

As her heart swelled and her eyes filled with tears, her gaze roved around the room, and she spotted the gifts underneath the Christmas tree.

When did they come? She hadn't brought any gifts. She hadn't even thought about gifts. She didn't have a single gift bought, and she wasn't sure she was going to get anything at this point.

Especially if she was going to be watching five children for the foreseeable future. She was sure that everyone would understand, and gifts had not even crossed her mind.

Except, there were gifts under her tree.

She looked around the room, trying to figure out who wasn't there. All of her kids were, and Jones sat with Amy.

Terry was with her in the kitchen, and... Judd was gone.

Casually, Marjorie walked down the hall and slipped into one of the bedrooms, looking outside.

At first, there was a cloud over the moon, and she couldn't see anything, but as her eyes adjusted to the light, and she continued to look, she saw a dark figure, one that looked suspiciously like Judd, with a bag over his shoulder, walking up the steps of the back porch. He would come in the door right by the tree, and if he came in quietly, no one in the living room would see because the tree would block the view. If she was working in the kitchen with her back to it, or even if she were looking into the living room, she would miss him.

She watched as he finished walking up the steps and slipped in the door.

She walked quietly back down the hall and stood in the doorway, just in the shadows, watching as he carefully pulled gifts out of the bag and set them up quickly around the tree before retreating back out the door.

He didn't even look to see if anyone was looking. He just did it quickly, and maybe he thought that that would be the saving grace.

So fast that no one noticed.

She thought about the articles that she'd read on social media. She hadn't seen them all, because who had time? But she'd seen a few. Written by Terry. Of all people.

Judd was the Secret Saint. She would almost bet on it.

Did Terry know Judd was the Secret Saint that she wrote about?

Surely she had to.

She'd seen them talking quietly together several times, and there seemed to be something between them.

She smiled. Pleased at how quickly God had answered her prayer. Sometimes a person had to wait a long time for an answer.

I needed some good news, Lord, and You came through, better than I could even have thought. Wow. Whether Judd is the Secret Saint or not, thank you for sending him to be with our family at this time. I know that the kids are going to be over-the-moon excited.

They had never done Santa Claus when her kids were little, and her kids had continued that non-tradition. She didn't judge people who did, but she just wanted to keep Christmas about Jesus. Making things look pretty, creating their own traditions, and knowing that God giving Jesus as His gift to mankind was the reason that they exchanged gifts with each other.

She set the meat and rolls out, along with condiments, in case someone wanted to make a sandwich, and then slipped into the living room, sitting down in the opening so that she could catch Landon if he thought to crawl out.

Isadora saw her and smiled her thanks.

"Excuse me," Judd said over her shoulder as he stepped into the living room.

"Of course," she said, trying not to smile any bigger at him than she normally would have.

It looked like he had just gone to the restroom, but she knew better. Although she didn't say anything.

"Before we sing something else, I wanted to make an announcement," Terry said, standing up and waiting for Judd to reach her side.

He stopped beside and put his arm around her, and she leaned into him, like...they were a couple.

Lord? More good news?

Marjorie could hardly contain herself. If this was what she thought it was, God had really outdone Himself.

Terry looked at Judd, and there seemed to be some kind of silent messaging going on between them before he nodded.

"I've asked Terry to marry me, and she said yes."

Conversation and cheers erupted in the living room as Terry's siblings congratulated her and showed their surprise.

Amy didn't look overly shocked, and Marjorie wondered if maybe Amy had known beforehand.

Amy and Jones were looking kind of cozy, but Amy didn't stand up with her own announcement.

"Now, for the really shocking news," Terry said, and the family groaned. What could be more shocking than that?

Marjorie held her breath. This could go either way. Good news or bad.

She would be happy about a baby, but she would be more happy if they were already married. It was just the way she felt about sin, but she wasn't going to rain on anyone's parade by giving a lecture on morality when an announcement about a new grandchild had been made.

The lectures on morality that she had given to her children were over and done with.

It was up to them to make their decisions about their lives and go to her for advice if they wanted it. She tried not to offer it unsolicited.

"Are you gonna tell us or not?" Roland asked, raising his voice to be heard above everyone else.

"Of course. So, Judd and I decided that we weren't going to sit around waiting with a long engagement. We're already in the same house, and it's not really set up like a duplex, and it makes both of us a little bit uncomfortable, so we decided to go Monday morning to get a license, and we're planning on getting married that evening around six o'clock at the church."

There was stunned silence.

Marjorie almost laughed. If she wanted to, she couldn't get her kids to be this quiet, and now all of a sudden, no one could think of anything to say. Not until Marissa said, "Does that mean Mr. Judd's going to be my uncle?"

"It sure does, sweetheart. Yours, Lucas's, Robert's, Landon's, and Jasper's." Marjorie named all five of her grandchildren. How had she become a grandmother? She felt like she was still in her twenties in her heart, although her body felt more her age.

But still, grandchildren? *Lord, You've been too good to me.* She looked around the room again, her heart full. Sure, there were hard times. Lots of them. But there were good, wonderful, amazing times, too. So, so many more.

"Do you have any other bombs to drop on us?" Wilson asked, sounding a little gruff, but he didn't fool anyone. He was happy for his sister.

"I think that's pretty much it for me, for us." They looked at each other, and Judd gave Terry such a look of love and admiration that Marjorie couldn't help but be excited. It would be a bit of a change, but not much. Although, Terry had come back thinking that she was going to help a lot around the house, but if she were in a new relationship, in a new marriage, she probably would want to focus on that, as well she should. Still, Marjorie figured she would see her around a lot more than she had when she'd been working two and a half hours away in Richmond.

There was more laughter, more good-natured teasing, and then the singing started again. This time, Marjorie joined in, playing with the children that came over to her and grateful that she was still young enough that she could get down on the floor with them.

She remembered her mom playing with her children when they were young, but at that time, her mom had been older and had not wanted to get down on the floor for fear that she couldn't get up. Marjorie had tried to stay active because she didn't want to have that problem with her own grandchildren.

She figured great-grandchildren might be a different story, but for now, God had given her the health that she needed to be able to help her children when they needed it. And that was all she could ask for.

Chapter Eighteen

Amy sat beside Jones in the wagon leading the children as they sang, while Judd and Terry sat on the bench behind them, driving the horses.

Terry didn't always come, but after yesterday, announcing to their family that they were going to get married, and today, when they had announced to the church that they were going to get married, she figured they wanted to spend as much time as possible together. There was just something beautiful about the engagement. And it was going to be short, so they might as well enjoy it.

Of course, hers and Jones's was going to be even shorter, but she didn't want to take away anything from Terry's happiness, even though Terry had said that she didn't care.

"How many of you ate your cookies from yesterday?" Jones asked the kids, and there was a chorus of voices as they answered, some with hands, some with stories, and all trying to talk over the others.

Jones had been so good with the kids, and this wagon idea with the horses had been an excellent one. It had given the horses a new lease on life, and it had given the kids something fun to do for the Christmas season. The wagon had been decked out like a sleigh, although she hadn't quite been able to get her mind to say sleigh instead of wagon, since she knew exactly what it was.

Still, she and Jones had a great time, and she didn't think there was going to be any doubt that they wanted to do it next year as long as Judd and Terry were willing and Belle and Bob were still available.

Although, maybe they could have a few special things throughout the year that would get them out and about, just to keep them in practice.

Lucas, Marissa, and Robert were all on the wagon, while her mom had taken Jasper and Landon home with her.

Isadora had not made it to church, and that hadn't surprised anyone. She was working through some really hard things, and Amy figured that if it were her, she might want to be around some familiar, happy faces, but she also might want to wait until she felt like she was able to handle it on her own before she talked to a lot of people about it. She honestly had been surprised that Isadora had shown up at the house yesterday.

Gilbert hadn't said much, but she thought that he appreciated not being alone. It had been after midnight before everyone had left, most of the food had been gone, and her mom had taken her aside and told her that Isadora had eaten.

Amy had been concerned about it, and Terry had been particularly worried.

Both of them were relieved to hear that.

Not just for Isadora, because Amy figured it was probably normal for someone who was going through something like she was to lose weight, but it was more because of the baby. They didn't want to add more tragedy on tragedy.

"Are you ready for our announcement?" Jones asked, allowing his fingers to trail through her hair.

She liked the way that felt, liked the way his voice rumbled in her ear, liked the way it felt sitting beside him and being able to touch his leg and hold his hand. Although they hadn't done that today, since she wanted to tell her family first.

"I'm actually excited about it," she said, turning to him and being sincere.

The wagon stopped, and they helped the two kids who lived in the house in front of them out, holding their papers and candy that they'd gotten at church.

They waved, and the kids waved back, and then the wagon pulled away and Jones started them on the first verse of "Hark! The Herald Angels Sing."

The kids joined in with gusto, because they'd trained them to sing from their hearts for the Lord. When they first started singing, no one had wanted to, and that might have partly been because no one knew the songs, but it also took some conditioning, since the kids were naturally reticent, and the idea of singing for Jesus was not one that was talked about a lot in even Christian homes, and most of these kids came from secular families.

She didn't know how much good they were doing, but she had heard success stories of children who had been brought to church either through buses or other means, who had grown up to serve the Lord and give Him their lives, and she could only hope that some of the kids that they were working with would do the same.

She wondered how that was possible, since she knew so many families who had Christian parents, whose children didn't turn out for the Lord. And weren't living a Christian life. What chance was there for a kid who hadn't grown up with parents to guide them of ever living for Jesus?

She knew that God had a lot to do with it, and she just prayed that His hand would be on the children that she loved and cared for so much.

They dropped the last kid off and said goodbye to Terry and Judd, who still had to unhook the horses and take them back to the farm before coming to her parents' house.

Lucas, Marissa, and Robert were going home with them since Gilbert hadn't been in church either. And despite the fact that

Marissa was in a princess dress, they raced each other to Jones's pickup, laughing and calling to each other.

Marissa had had a breakdown in Sunday school, and Robert had had a meltdown before they'd even gotten to Sunday school, but it looked like they were all doing fine now. Even Lucas was smiling.

"Did you see someone managed to get the gifts under the tree last night?"

"I did," Amy said as they walked well behind the children. Not holding hands.

But they were walking close enough that they could talk low even though there wasn't anyone left other than the pastor and chatty folks, who still hadn't made it out of the building yet, and their arms brushed occasionally.

"I can't believe that they were able to do it without me seeing. I was watching for it! But I went out to get a sandwich, then they were there!"

"I tried to keep an eye out for him, but then we started singing, and I didn't even think about it."

"He's good at what he does, that's for sure," she said, then they shared a knowing glance as Jones went to her side of the truck and opened the door for her. The kids were already in the back.

"Thank you," she said, giving him a smile. He touched her arm and then let his fingers trail down and grab her hand quickly for a squeeze before he said, "My pleasure," and shut her door.

It was crazy the way he could make her tingle and she hadn't even thought about it before. But the look in his eyes, the tone of his voice, the trail of his fingers, it definitely made her heart beat faster and her mind feel like mush.

She wanted to tell him not to do that to her, but she actually kind of liked it.

They drove to her parents' house and got out. Amy hadn't made anything because their house was full of leftovers and meat trays that people had dropped off because of Gilbert and because of Sally's passing.

The kids hopped out and ran in the house, and she and Jones smiled into each other's eyes as they walked up the sidewalk. They did not hold hands, but Amy told herself that it could be the last time they ever walked up the sidewalk not holding hands.

She knew that was probably unreasonable. There would be plenty of times where they might have kids or packages or maybe they would even be angry at each other, although... She hoped not. She hoped they could continue the friendship that they'd had, the one that was respectful and kind and where they understood each other and didn't get angry about dumb things that didn't matter.

He opened the door for her, and she walked in, eager to tell her family her good news.

Chapter Nineteen

Jones waited until everyone was seated at the table, after they said grace, and after the food had been passed. Marjorie had heated up a casserole that they had gotten yesterday for dinner. It smelled good, though he doubted it would be as good as Marjorie's cooking. She had a real talent in that area, and there weren't too many things she made that he didn't love.

There had been vegetables left over, and they'd made fresh dill pickle dip, and it was on the table as well. Another one of his favorites. He didn't even need vegetables; he could eat just the dip. Although, if he did that, Amy would elbow him and tell him that it was weird, and they'd end up in a squabbling match that Marjorie would have to regulate, except they'd be laughing too, and they'd all be joking.

They'd done that plenty of times over the years, as the dip had become a staple as soon as Marjorie realized it was his favorite.

She'd been like a mom to him, far more of a mom than his own mom, and yet his mom knew that he was planning on getting married before Marjorie. And if Marjorie knew that, she wouldn't be upset at all. Because that was just the kind of woman she was. She understood that not everybody could be first, and she was happy taking a place at the back.

He admired that about her and knew Amy was like that as well. She didn't always have to be first, although it made him smile when he remembered how she had told him that he better not tell anybody else if he wasn't going to tell her, and he knew that was partly because she wanted to be special to him. Not like she didn't already know that she was. She surely did, but he understood. When you told someone else something first, it made it seem like they were more important.

Regardless, he took a breath, then pushed his chair back away from the table and stood up. When he just stood there, everyone looked at him.

Even Isadora, who had come for lunch, and Gilbert, who had come out of his room as well, though neither one of them had been at church.

"I have an announcement," he said, and immediately he saw Marjorie's eyes widen. "It's a good one, I think."

He looked down at Amy, who looked around the table and then stood up, looking at him and smiling.

"You guys are getting married too!" Roland called out.

"Welp, yep. That was my announcement," Jones said, nodding at Roland. "Thanks for making it easy for me there, bro," he said, not upset at all. Roland was the youngest of six, and Jones had often figured that he felt like he got lost in the crowd. It was probably true he did. Even now that he was an adult, he probably still felt that way at times, like nothing he did was ever matching anything that anyone else did. Jones actually remembered having several conversations with him about that when Roland was still in high school. He just felt...like he never stood out for himself.

Jones made a note to try to talk to him later. It was probably overwhelming to lose a sister-in-law, have a sister lose her husband, and then have two sisters get married. He might be feeling the same. And while Jones wasn't exactly sure what to do about it, he could at least reach out. See if he thought of anything, or he could chat with him for a bit, make sure he was okay.

"Congratulations!" Marjorie said, breaking the silence that had descended, maybe from shock.

That seemed to be the instigation that everyone needed, and chatter broke out around the table, with congratulations and questions called from different ends of the table.

Jones put a hand up. "You guys know that Amy and I have been good friends forever, and there's a little bit more to the story."

He and Amy had talked about it and decided that it would be best for them to just be straight-up honest about the reasons for getting married. They had also decided that they weren't going to give a figure on the money that he was inheriting, just so that that little bit remained private.

"You guys can keep eating if you want to, I didn't want to hold up the meal, but we wanted to tell you for a reason." He looked around the table, then at Amy. She was going to tag team with him, he was pretty sure.

"It started with the mistletoe kiss for me. That was your fault, Robert." She smiled down at her nephew, sitting at the other end of the table. "You are the one who brought the mistletoe over, and Jones kissed me. That...got me thinking. I had never thought of him like that before."

"That was pretty fast. Because that was Friday," Wilson said, not looking upset but still sounding surprised.

"I know. But we've been friends for years. I know him better than anyone. He knows me better than anyone, and it just seemed natural, once we started talking about it."

"And I know your mom knows that we got a letter saying that one of my aunts had died and left us money, and it said that I would inherit money from her, but I had to be married. I was looking for someone to marry, and Amy was helping me. Until that moment, I hadn't really considered that Amy would be the perfect one. But after that, it was obvious."

"Yeah. We all knew it," Gilbert said, and Jones figured that was probably a good thing that he was at least invested in this and it didn't seem to be making him feel bad. Maybe it wasn't going to be hard for him to hear.

"Anyway, you're right. It was obvious to everyone but us. But the other stipulation in the will was that it had to be within one month of her dying. That's Friday." There were gasps around the table.

"I talked to Terry, and we found out that we were both thinking about getting married soon, and we said why don't we do it together?"

"So you're getting married tomorrow too?" Marjorie said, her hands at her throat.

"I'm sorry if that bothers you, Mom. Normally I would ask for your advice, but it doesn't feel like there's any choice in the matter."

"It doesn't bother me at all!" she said. "Why would it bother me? I'm thrilled for you guys!"

"Well, there's not going to be any wedding to plan, obviously. We're just going to go to the church tomorrow and get married. It's not going to be a big deal, and it's just going to be the family, although Jones's parents are invited as well."

No one had anything to say about that. They all knew how his parents could be. They might show up, but they probably wouldn't.

"Well, we have all this food that everybody's been bringing, and now we have a reason to eat it and celebrate. You could invite people from the church to come over after you're married, for a better reception if you want," Gilbert said, and Jones almost swallowed his tongue.

Gilbert was almost acting like...he had forgotten that his wife died. Or maybe he just needed to. Maybe he needed to be like the kids and have periods of normalcy followed by periods of deep sadness. Jones didn't really know, but he appreciated the fact that Gilbert had volunteered, and he would no more have turned him down than he would have cut off his own arm.

"Does that sound good to you guys?" Amy asked Terry and Judd, who nodded, smiling.

"Any excuse to eat sounds like a good thing to me," Judd said, and the table laughed.

"Well, there we have it. It's settled. We'll be getting married tomorrow evening, around six. We all have to get off work and get to the church."

"It's a good thing too, because there's a storm coming on Tuesday. Although, they have been calling for twelve inches of snow, but now they're saying it's going to be an ice storm."

Jones hadn't heard that. There were too many other things going on, and he hadn't checked the weather lately. "Thank you. I might end up closing my clinic for Tuesday."

"You'd close your clinic for an ice storm, but you won't close it for our marriage?" Amy said, putting a hand on her hip.

"Really, darling? In front of your family?"

It sounded so fake that the entire table laughed. It was probably going to take people a while to get used to Amy and him being more than just bantering friends. But he didn't care. It had taken him a little bit of time too, but now that he had, he couldn't think of anything that would be better.

Chapter Twenty

onday morning dawned, clear, bright, and cool. Isadora told Amy she was going back to their mom's house, because of Amy's upcoming nuptials, knowing that they were probably going to live in Amy's house, which was correct.

Her mom had promised that she would watch the children, and Isadora could have as much time to herself as she needed, although Amy could see the worry in her mother's eyes when she said that.

Still, Amy couldn't deny that she did appreciate it, since she'd spent Saturday night on her mom's couch, and it was nice to be back in her own bed.

She took the sheets off when she got up and threw them in the washer before putting her clothes on and going outside.

Jones was already at work feeding the dogs.

It wasn't unusual, exactly, for him to get there before her, but she wondered if maybe he was a little nervous.

She saw a steaming coffee cup sitting on the nearest post to the house, and she grabbed it as she walked around the kennel, petting some wet noses and taking a sip of the strong coffee which warmed her the whole way to her stomach and back.

"Good morning," she said, smiling at Jones as he carried the bucket down the aisle, putting the correct amount of dog food in each automatic feeder.

"Hey there, beautiful. It's your wedding day."

"I know. And the groom isn't supposed to see the bride on their wedding day, is he?"

"If you believe that, you should have stayed inside when you saw my truck out here."

"And let you do all the work? That sounds like more bad luck than you seeing me." She didn't believe in luck at all, but if she did, she certainly would think it would be more important to help him than to stay hidden somewhere.

"Well, I have to say I appreciate the fact that you think that way. Since that'll make this morning a little easier for me."

"No doubt," she agreed, grabbing her own scoop, going down, and giving him a hand with every other dog.

"You know, it's occurred to me that maybe we do this backward. Perhaps you should think about cleaning their pens before you feed them."

"I used to do it that way. But I found that if I feed them first, they're more likely to poop on their walk, and it saves me a little bit of work in cleaning things up. Plus, it gives them a new place to mark as their territory, or whatever they do," she said.

He nodded. Then she figured he was making conversation because he really was nervous. She wasn't quite sure what to do about that though. She was nervous too.

"You know, we really didn't talk about where we were going to stay after our wedding, and it's okay with me if I don't even move in." He didn't look at her while he was talking, and she wondered if maybe he was changing his mind about something.

"Do you want to move in?" she asked, pausing with the scoop in her hands, hoping that that wasn't the wrong question, and hoping that it was a question that she could ask and expect an honest answer to. He'd always been very forthright with her, and she didn't think that he had changed, but maybe she was wrong.

"I want to," he said quickly, before she could think of too much else. "But I just thought that maybe you were uncomfortable."

"I'm uncomfortable. But you're right, we haven't really talked about it. Because if you move in... I only have one bedroom."

"Right. And your couch is not even big enough for you to sleep on. So, I didn't want to do anything that was going to make you uncomfortable. I mean, this is all kind of new, and I don't know that we're ready to take that next step yet."

He was right. It wasn't really a next step. It was more like an impossible leap.

"Why can't we just put pillows or something down the middle of the bed, and you sleep on one side, and I'll sleep on the other, and I don't think it will be that big of a deal. I mean, we can keep it from being that big of a deal. Can't we?"

After she said that, she felt like they were in charge. They didn't have to go with what someone else said, and they didn't have to go with their feelings either. They could make the decisions using logic and compassion.

"Are you sure about that? That won't make you uncomfortable or anything?" He paused. "We'd be sharing the bathroom."

"But it has a door on it. I mean, I think eventually we'll be perfectly comfortable with each other, but there's no point in getting all hurried and crazy. We can just take it naturally," she said. Not sure exactly what naturally was, but knowing that eventually they would be comfortable enough with each other that it wouldn't matter whether there was a door in the bathroom or not. She hoped so. That was the way most married couples were, wasn't it?

It wasn't something she went around asking people, and she figured that maybe married couples each had their own thing. Maybe some did, some didn't, they just did what worked for them.

"You think you'd be comfortable enough with me to share the bathroom at some point?" he asked, like he could read her thoughts.

"Well, I was just thinking about that, and it occurred to me that if we're going to have children, and I assume we are at some point," she was proud of herself for not even blushing over that one, "you're probably going to want to see our baby be born. And if I can't share the bathroom with you, that might be awkward. So… Yeah. And it's not just me. You too."

"I see. So you're not scared?"

"Should I be?" Then she laughed. "Never mind. I've been around when you're going to the bathroom before, and you're right. I probably ought to be scared. Maybe that might be taking it a bit too far."

It was his turn to laugh, and he knew she was joking.

For her, marriage meant everything. Not just the things that made a person comfortable.

But because they were doing this in an uncommonly fast way, they didn't have to do everything right away.

"All right. Then I suppose I ought to pack my shaving kit and some clothes and the stuff that I'd need if I were going to be gone for a few days, and put them in my truck, and bring them here after the wedding."

"Or I can do it. You have to go to work, and I have a few errands to run, more dog food to get, but I can definitely go to your house. Plus, I don't think you want that stuff sitting in your car all day, because the temperatures are supposed to drop pretty sharply."

"Yeah. I saw they are supposed to get below freezing."

"Wilson said that he would come out and feed the dogs in the morning so that we can sleep in if you want to. But I figured if you're going to go to work, I might as well get up and feed the dogs, but I thought I would talk to you about it before I replied to his text."

"Let him come. I'm going to have Cheryl, my secretary, call and cancel all appointments tomorrow. Whether we get stormy weather or we don't, you are right. How can I think of canceling for a storm when I wouldn't cancel for my marriage?"

"I was kidding," she said as they walked back to fill their buckets full of dog food again.

"I know. But it just made me think. Also, we need to take a honeymoon. So pick your dates, and I'll clear my calendar."

"I don't need a honeymoon," she said.

"If we're getting the ten million dollars, we might as well spend it on something good."

"A clinic for you," she said emphatically.

"And dog kennels for you," he said, making sure she wasn't going to leave herself out of the equation.

"And if we're going to have children, we should probably add on to the house or build one." She paused. "But nothing fancy."

"You got me with the nothing fancy. I'm totally fine with that."

They finished feeding the dogs, chatting about that evening, and the fact that they needed to go get a license over his lunch break, and nothing else urgent, until it was time for him to go.

She watched him drive away, knowing that she would see him again in a few hours, when they went to get their license. They had been going to drive along with Terry and Judd, but both of them needed to get back to their clinics, and their lunch breaks were half an hour different, so they didn't want to take a chance of one of them not making it.

Amy walked back to the house, unable to believe that today was her wedding day.

Chapter Twenty-One

They got the licenses without incident, and Amy decided that she would do the unusual thing of taking a bath rather than a quick shower, after she made their bed, and take her time getting ready for the wedding.

She just had one nice dress, and it wasn't exactly a Christmas dress, but she put it on anyway. It would look more like spring than winter, and with a storm coming the next day, she felt a little foolish, but she found a sweater that didn't look too bad with it and decided that she'd rather have a pretty dress on and be a little bit chilly than wear a sweater and a skirt and feel a little underdressed for her own wedding.

She finished her bath, got the bed made, and had gotten her dress on, and she was in the process of blow-drying her hair, when there was a frantic knock at the door.

It was a little before five, and at first, she thought it might be Jones, but then she realized he wouldn't have made it back from the clinic yet. He had said he had patients up until five, so he might be a little bit late. They were planning on riding together so that they wouldn't have two vehicles at the church.

"Amy! Amy!"

She recognized her sister Terry, and she sounded panicked.

She ran to the door, yanking it open.

Her sister spoke before she could say anything. "We found a dog alongside the road. It's been hit. It doesn't have a collar on, and I'm pretty sure its leg is fractured... I know that we're supposed to be going to our wedding, but Judd and I just couldn't drive by."

"Of course not," Amy said emphatically. "Take it to the clinic, I'll follow in my car, and I'll text Jones. As far as I know, he's still there."

"All right. I'm so glad I got off work a little bit early. We were able to move it off the road and into my car, and otherwise... I don't know what would have happened to him. Maybe there are internal injuries. I don't know."

"Just go. I'll be right there." They didn't say how they had gotten the dog in or whether it was even conscious.

Amy grabbed her phone off the bathroom sink where she had left it and texted Jones on her way through, shoving her feet in her boots and feeling even more ridiculous with her pretty white flowing dress and her muck boots coming out underneath.

She grabbed her heavy coat, threw her arms in the sleeves, and checked her phone to see if Jones had texted her back.

Bring it.

That was all she needed to see.

She knew he would say that. And he knew that she would be there to help him. He would probably let his regular help go home.

He might have left the clinic. He didn't say. But he would be turning around immediately and getting the operating table sanitized and ready.

She drove so fast, she caught up to Terry and Judd as they pulled into the clinic.

Barely waiting until her car was stopped, she jumped out and ran up to their car.

"How is he?" she asked as Terry got out of the front. She didn't want to open the back door in case it was awake and scared and tried to get out.

"We have a towel underneath it. I just did laundry for Isadora, and Judd put it in my car so I could give it back to her today, and unfortunately, I...used a few of her towels. We wrapped his face in one, so he wouldn't bite us. It was hurting him, and he was struggling a good bit."

"I see. Good thoughts. Sorry about Isadora's towels."

She supposed, if the ten million dollars really did materialize, they could probably replace Isadora's towels, but she also knew that her sister wouldn't mind donating them for such a good cause.

Jones moved to her side, his hand resting lightly on her back. "Let me in. I can get a hold of him, if Judd can reach in and hold the towel that has his head in it."

"All right. I'll go open the door and hold it for you guys so you can go right in." Then she gave Judd quick directions to get to the operating room. The clinic wasn't that big and wasn't complicated.

She opened the door and held it as they practically followed her in. Jones spoke as they maneuvered in the door. "I was just locking up for the night. Everyone else is gone." He paused. "I'm going to need you."

Then, he noticed that she had her old coat on over the top of her pretty white and blue dress and her muck boots.

"You look...interesting. I might have been a little stunned as you walked down the aisle."

She allowed the door to close and hurried after them, walking beside Terry. "This was not what I was wearing to the wedding."

"I know, but it's so much fun to tease you."

They grinned at each other over the squirming bundle, and she knew that he enjoyed it, and she loved that he did. Even at a time like this, where she felt like every second was imperative, and she was concerned about the welfare of the dog, she liked that he was able to keep things light enough so that she didn't get lost in her head.

They made it into the operating theater. Jones didn't have a whole lot of fancy equipment, but he did have a portable X-ray machine, which he had gotten set up.

Jones started murmuring low, describing what he was going to do.

He paused for a moment, and Terry said, "If you don't mind, I'm going to text the pastor and our family and just tell them everything that is going on here." She paused, then added, "And we'll just get married here, if that's okay."

Amy blinked and met Jones's gaze over the whimpering dog. He gave a slight shrug.

"Sure. That's fabulous." It wasn't in her plan, but since they didn't have a whole lot of plans, it wasn't that hard to adjust her mindset. "Thank you."

And then, as Terry turned to leave, Amy added, "Would you text Jones's parents, please? I don't know if they're planning on coming. I haven't heard from them." She looked at Jones, who shook his head and lifted a shoulder before looking back down at the dog and paying attention to what he was doing.

"Of course. I have her number. Don't worry about it. We'll be in the waiting room if you need us."

"Thank you," she said and turned back to Jones. "Thank you for doing this. I'm sorry I screwed up our wedding."

"You didn't screw it up. You made it so that it's totally a part of what you and I do."

"I didn't mean to, but I guess it worked out."

They worked on the dog for forty minutes or so, until Terry came to the door and said that everyone was crowded in the waiting room and any time that they could take a break, the pastor was ready to do the nuptials.

Jones finished up what he was doing and then looked at the dog. "I think he'll be stable until we get back. I hate to tell the pastor to hurry, but... I might."

For some reason, that made Amy want to giggle. "I think he'll understand," she said. "Or we could just have him do the vows in here, while we work."

"That would probably be the weirdest wedding he's ever officiated, wouldn't it?"

"Well, your choice."

"I think I want to hold your hand while I say my vows. If that's okay with you. He'll be okay here."

"All right. That sounds good."

She had blood on her dress. Jones had changed into a button-down shirt and dress pants before he left the clinic, and they were covered in blood as well. Neither one of them had taken the time to put a lab coat on.

But it was okay, the clothes were expendable, but the dog's life was not.

"Shall we?" he asked, pulling his gloves off and holding out his hand for her.

"Yeah. Let's do it."

"Also, before I forget, I think you should become a vet tech. When we build our new facility, we'll just put a nursery right beside the operating room, which also will face the back of the receptionist area, and we'll both be able to see the kids wherever we are, and we'll be in here together every day."

"That's about the best idea I've heard in a long time."

"Better than the idea of marrying me?" he asked, and maybe there was a note of insecurity in his tone, she wasn't quite sure. Regardless, it wasn't necessary for it to be there.

"No. That's the best idea I've ever had."

"Hold up there. Kiddo. I'm pretty sure that was my idea."

"No way. It was mine. All the way. I don't even know why you're trying to take the credit. You would never in a million years have thought of it."

"That's not the slightest bit true. I was on the verge of figuring this out, and I was going to—"

"Guys. Maybe not on your wedding day." Marjorie stood, her

hands full, holding one grandchild on her hip and holding the hand of another one beside her, but still, she had that mothering look that she used on both Amy and Jones to good effect.

"Sorry, Mom," Jones said.

"He started it," Amy said.

And everyone laughed.

Terry and Judd were already at the makeshift altar, with the pastor standing beyond them, so Amy and Jones made their way there and stood in front of the pastor.

"You ready?" The pastor looked at both couples.

They all nodded, and the service began.

Amy had been to more romantic weddings. She'd been to weddings with a better message. She probably had even been to weddings where the decorations had been more sparse, but she had never been to a wedding with more love in the room. And she figured that was the most important thing.

Chapter Twenty-Two

"Thanks for taking care of the dog today." Amy sat at the table where they'd eaten their wedding supper. It had been food that their mother had given them from the stash that people had been bringing to her.

But they didn't mind leftovers. It was nice to not have to cook.

"You knew I'd do it. No problem. It's my job."

"I know. You never even questioned me."

"Because it's you, Amy. You're special."

He knew she knew that, or at least he thought he did, but he wanted her to be sure of it. He might be kind to other people, but it wasn't the same. Amy held a special place in his life, as well as his heart. He would do anything for her, anything at all. And that made her different from his other friends.

It was late, after nine. They'd wanted the dog to be stable and awake from surgery before they left him.

They might even get up in the middle of the night and go check, or just leave early in the morning. Jones hadn't decided yet.

It might depend on the ice storm too.

"I hope you can get to the clinic in the morning."

"If I can't, the couple I'm renting the garage from said they would go out and check. Also, they told me that they had an offer on their house. They said that if they accepted it, closing would be in sixty days."

"Wow. That's...February."

"I know. I don't know if we can get another clinic set up in that amount of time or not. If not, I might have to shut down for a little bit. That might be a good time for us to go on a honeymoon."

"You're set on this honeymoon idea," she said as she stood, gathering up the plates and taking them to the kitchen. Which was only a step and a half away. She looked tired, weary, her dress sad and dirty, but she was still beautiful in his eyes. He couldn't believe it, his best friend. He was married to her.

"You know what your house is lacking," he said as he looked around before carrying the casserole dish to the counter and grabbing the aluminum foil and putting some over the top of it.

"Tell me. What is my house lacking?" she said with a little bit of sarcasm in her voice like she knew it was lacking a lot.

"It's lacking a Christmas tree. And any Christmas decorations. If I came into this house and I didn't know you, I would think you were some kind of Scrooge."

"Wow. That's harsh," she said, pretending to shudder.

"It's the truth. I think first thing tomorrow, or actually, when the roads are passable and it's not dangerous to drive, you and I need to go get a Christmas tree."

"I can't believe the Secret Saint didn't give us one. Didn't he know that I didn't have one?"

"Maybe he didn't think you were needy enough. Or maybe he thought you have a man who's supposed to provide for you and should provide you with a Christmas tree."

"Now there's a thought," she said, smiling.

"I'm serious. We need to get a tree."

"All right. I'm down for that." Amy spoke easily like it didn't matter to her whether they got a tree or not, or more likely, she was willing to go along with it because he thought of it.

"What about tomorrow?"

"Isn't that a little bit hypocritical?" she asked as she ran some water in the sink to wash dishes.

He grabbed a tea towel as he shrugged a shoulder. "How so?"

"If you close your clinic because of the storm, then you drive to get a Christmas tree, wouldn't that look...bad?"

"I'm closing the clinic for people so they don't feel like they have to get there and have an accident on the way. It's for them, not me."

That seemed perfectly reasonable, but Amy snorted, and he figured she probably knew he was being slightly sarcastic.

"All right. That's a decent explanation. We'll go get a tree tomorrow."

She handed him a plate, and their fingers brushed.

He caught his breath. What was wrong with him? He'd touched Amy plenty of times before. But he found himself staring at her, as she turned nonchalantly back to the sink like she didn't feel a thing.

It was an awkward few seconds before he remembered he was supposed to be drying the plate, and started to rub it with his tea towel. What had they been talking about?

He couldn't remember, but he wanted to talk about something completely different. Like what they were going to be doing tonight. They'd had that conversation about dividing the bed in two so each of them got a side, but they also said that they wanted to have a real marriage. Was she thinking they would have a real marriage tonight?

The idea sent a sliver of excitement down his spine, and something sweet and warm chimed in his stomach. He castigated himself for wanting to focus on that, but they were married, and that was the natural progression of things.

She was finished washing the next plate before he was done drying the first one, and she waited, plate in hand, giving him a concerned glance.

"Are you okay?"

This time when he took the plate from her, he was careful not to brush her fingers. He wasn't sure what was going to be going on, but it had to be nothing, and he ought to at least try to control himself. That would be easier to do if he wasn't touching her. Crazy. Since this was Amy, his best friend.

"Yeah. I'm fine. Why?" he finally said, noticing that he sounded breathless. The idea that Amy might not notice was laughable.

"You sound funny," she said, turning back to the sink and burying her hands in the water.

He was making everything awkward, and he hated that.

"Did I make you feel guilty for not being at the clinic? Because, I'm not upset about that at all. I was just teasing you."

"I know you were. And no. I don't feel guilty. I don't feel guilty about that or about spending time with my new bride."

She laughed. The forks clanked as she used the rag to wipe them off. "That's crazy isn't it? Who would've ever thought?"

"I think there are a lot of people who thought you and I were just a little slow on the uptake."

"Well, we speeded up quite nicely in the last few weeks, even if I do say so myself."

"That we did." He wanted to keep going fast, but he didn't want to say that and push her into something she wasn't ready for. But how did he ask her if she was ready? If she wanted to be more than friends with him? Maybe she wasn't thinking any such thing. Maybe she was thinking about the money.

That's probably what he should be thinking about, and getting it as soon as he could just so she could get out of debt and breathe a little easier.

"So do you or don't you want to do the Christmas tree tomorrow?" he asked, finally deciding that he'd just change the subject. He tried to stop thinking about kissing her, and not make it so awkward that they had trouble remembering that they were supposed to be friends, friends who were married, and he could let things take their natural course. When Amy was ready, she'd make a move. It was probably better for him to wait for her.

"I do. I'm kind of excited about it. And it would be nice to have some Christmas cheer, not that our wedding wasn't a happy time, but if we have the house decorated after the funeral, it will be nice to come back to."

"Agreed."

He'd kind of forgotten about the funeral. Amy was right. It would be nice to have a cheerful home to come back to, after the sadness of putting a mother of young children and the wife of someone he considered family to rest. Even if she was celebrating in heaven. That must be what Amy was thinking about, and here he was thinking about other things, unable to focus on the needs of others or being considerate because he was so busy thinking about what he wanted.

Maybe he should cut himself a little bit of slack, because he was hardly the first bridegroom to spend his wedding day thinking about that.

The water swished as she pulled the plug out of the drain, and brought out the rag she had used.

"I'm exhausted," she said as she set the rag down on the counter. "Sorry I'm not very good company."

"I wanted to tell you that you should go to bed. You look tired and it's my job to take care of you."

There. That marked the change in their relationship. They took care of each other before. But, in marriage, the man was supposed to be the protector. He wanted to be someone she could depend on to take care of her.

"All right. Then I'll shower first?" She turned and looked at him, and he couldn't read anything in her eyes. He thought she had mentioned taking a bath earlier, and it seemed odd that she would take a shower the same day, although after taking care of the dog, with all the blood...maybe she just felt like she needed it. Maybe he shouldn't be reading anything into it at all.

"Sure. You shower, and I'll wipe the table and think about where we can put the Christmas tree."

"There aren't too many places. You'll have to get a little one."

"Last time I picked out a tree with you for your mother, it took three hours until you found the tree that you wanted. Maybe I should reconsider what I want to do tomorrow."

"You had a good time," she said, lifting a brow at him, and putting one hand on her hip.

"I thought you were showering." He made shooing motions with his hands, but she shook her head. "You're not fooling me. You had a good time and now you don't want to admit it."

"I did. That's what we do. I always have a good time with you."

Maybe he wasn't supposed to be serious. Maybe they were supposed to continue their bantering, but he meant that with all his heart. It didn't matter what they were doing, if he was doing it with Amy, he knew he would enjoy himself.

"Whether it's fixing up a dog, on our wedding day no less, or picking out a Christmas tree, or even standing in front of my parents having the most awkward conversation ever. It's always better when it's with you."

"I'm the same," she said. And he was a little disappointed, but then she continued. "Everything's better when I'm with you."

She turned and walked into the bedroom, while he grabbed the rag to go wipe the table. By the time he was done with his shower she had gotten some pillows and put them down the middle of the bed. She lay on her side of the bed, looking up at him with worried eyes.

"Is this okay?" she asked, jerking her head and indicating the pillows that split the bed in two.

"That's what we said we were going to do," he said easily. Reminding himself of what he had said earlier — that he was going to let Amy take the lead and he would follow her.

"All right. I tried to make it so that your side was a little bit bigger, since you're bigger than I am."

"I can fit just fine. I want you to be comfortable," he said, pausing at the light switch. "Is it okay if I shut it off?"

"Yeah. I should have a lamp beside my bed, but I guess I never felt like this was a place I was going to stay at forever and I just did the minimum."

He flipped the light off, careful to keep his face neutral until the room was plunged into darkness. He didn't want her to know that he was disappointed.

"That's perfectly fine. It's not that hard to shut the light off and get in bed."

"Normally it's me, and I hate that you had to do it."

"Not that big a deal, I promise." He sat down on the bed, and then lifted the blankets, carefully stretching out on his side, and not touching pillows at all.

There was less room than what it looked like there was going to be. The bed would be cozy if they were sharing it together.

He had been encouraged as she left the kitchen that they both agreed that everything they did was better if they did it together. But, he supposed that wasn't romantic in any way. It was just talking about good friends.

"Thanks a lot for today." Amy's voice came out of the darkness.

"For the dog? It's my job; you know I love that kind of stuff."

"And for marrying me. It wasn't very...romantic. Do men dream about their weddings?"

He huffed out a laugh. "Just the wedding night."

She laughed a little, and he wished he wouldn't have said that. It was way too close to what he was thinking about right now.

"You know you've always been a good example to me." Her voice was soft, almost as though she were thinking.

He wasn't the slightest bit sleepy, and welcomed a conversation.

"I thought it was the other way around. After all, you share your family. You taught me how to be a good sibling, even though I didn't have any. Then you showed me, by letting me see your parents, what a mom and dad should really be like."

"No. I meant you. Being selfless. Just always thinking about others. We were laughing a little earlier about you closing your clinic for other people so they didn't get hurt, rather than you, but that's really true. That's the kind of person you are. You put others first the way Jesus did. It's inspiring."

He hadn't realized she thought that. They'd never even spoken about it before, and he had no idea that she'd been watching him.

"You do the same thing. Although, I suppose you do it with animals."

"Maybe I treat animals better than I treat people?" She mused thoughtfully.

"Is there a problem with that?"

"The Bible doesn't really tell us how we have to treat animals other than regarding their life. But it is people who are made in the image of God. I don't know whether animals go to heaven, or what happens to them, and the Bible doesn't really tell us, but it's very clear about people. That's who Jesus came to save. That's who we're supposed to be reaching. Animals are just... I don't know."

"Companions. Something to make us smile. The way God gave us beautiful sunshine after a rainstorm, or rainbows, or the way the trees start to change color in the fall and we just can't help but look at them all and smile. Only, animals can be a companion too. They help our loneliness, help people feel better, give us something to snuggle with and something that doesn't judge us. Maybe when people get to be too much, you always have an animal around to try to make you feel better."

"Yeah. But maybe sometimes I elevate them into something that they shouldn't be. And I lose sight of what's really important. Even though your job is to take care of animals. You never lose sight of what's really the most important."

He didn't say anything, because he supposed she was probably right. He became a veterinarian because he loved animals. He and Amy both did. And they talked often when they were younger about how they wanted to work together, her as a vet tech, and him as the veterinarian. Not that she couldn't have been a veterinarian if she wanted to, she just hated to go to school.

It wasn't his favorite either, but he'd loved the idea of him and Amy being together.

"Anyway, I just wanted you to know that." Amy shifted, and he thought she was turning on her side. Soon he heard her deep, regular breathing, and he figured she was asleep.

It was a long time before he was able to do the same.

Chapter Twenty-Three

*I*t wasn't quite what she was expecting, Amy thought, as she flipped the pancakes on the griddle the next morning. Jones had braved the four inches of snow that had fallen to drive to the clinic to check on the dog he'd operated on the night before.

The snow had stopped, and it was beautiful outside. What a wonderful sight to wake up to on her first day of being married. Except she really didn't feel married, and she wasn't sure how Jones felt about her, and that bothered her more than what she thought it was going to.

She stuck the spatula underneath the pancake and flipped it, putting it on a plate, and carefully pouring more batter on the griddle.

She had decided that she would just let Jones take the lead, but she had been hoping that he would... Do something. Kiss her, or something.

But maybe he just didn't feel like that with her. Maybe all they ever would be was friends. Maybe she'd developed this huge crush on him, tingling when he touched her, barely able to keep from jerking her fingers back when they accidentally brushed while they were doing dishes. *Doing dishes* of all things.

It was crazy. She had to get a hold of herself, since Jones seemed to be perfectly okay.

He hadn't said much while they'd been feeding the dogs that morning, and before he left he just said that he was still planning on getting a Christmas tree if it was okay with her.

She nodded and said she'd cook breakfast.

Just mundane things, that would make her feel more married than ever, except...

He came back not long afterwards, reporting that the dog was doing as well as could have been expected, and they ate without talking too much.

The Christmas tree farm wasn't open when they got there, but by the time they picked out a tree and cut it down Amy knew that they would be open, so they parked, and strolled down through the field.

"I've always liked blue spruce." Jones shoved his hands in his pockets and walked beside her, the way he always had.

She nodded. "I know that's your favorite kind. In the past I haven't gotten them because they seem to dry out faster than other kinds, but since it's so close to Christmas it probably isn't going to matter unless we're going to keep our tree up through Valentine's Day or something."

"I was just kind of wondering how we're going to have room to live until Christmas. I can't imagine having it up through Valentine's Day, but if that's what you want."

She laughed. Knowing that he really wouldn't care. Even if they had to step over the top of each other for two months just so she could keep a Christmas tree up.

"That's one of the things I really like about you." She almost said "love." That's one of the things she *loved* about him. She stopped herself just in time.

"What's that?" he asked, not noticing her stumble.

"That you're just so easy-going. You don't get excited about stuff, and you don't have nasty little comments to say underneath your breath every time I want to do something. And not just with me. With anyone."

"There are people who do that, aren't there?"

"Men and women. It's not just men."

"I didn't think you were picking on my gender."

"No. It's just… Some people just don't seem to be able to be nice no matter how hard they try."

"Usually those are the people who don't seem to be trying very hard."

"True," she said, "Why is that? Why do some people just always seem to blame everyone else for everything?"

"I don't know. I mean, beyond the biblical commands that we're supposed to focus on the positive, it just doesn't feel very good to constantly be looking at other people and seeing things you don't like. Especially if you're married to them."

"Yeah. Now you need to be doubly sure to look at me and see only the good."

"Isn't that what we need to do? Especially with ourselves, but with anyone. You look at them through a lens of acceptance and love." He paused. "Not saying that we have to accept sin. But we get so confused about mixing up the fact that a person is still a person whether they're sinning or not."

"But if they're deliberately sinning, even God says they need to stop."

"He would, yeah. But even just common everyday interactions. How often do we roll our eyes, even if we're doing it privately, in exasperation at what someone else is doing? And we never seem to have the same exasperation over ourselves."

"We give ourselves all the grace we need, but we have a very limited supply when it comes to someone else."

"Yeah."

They were quiet for a little as the snow crunched under their feet. It was still cloudy overhead, but Amy knew from experience that the snow most likely would not last long. Because of their high elevation, Mistletoe Meadows got more snow than surrounding parts of Virginia, but maybe it was the angle of the sun, or maybe just their position further south, but it usually didn't last.

"Remember when it would snow when we were kids?" she asked, smiling at the good times they'd had.

"And we'd run outside and make a snowman as fast as we could before it melted? I remember. And your mom was always really awesome at making hot chocolate. Even if it got into the forties or fifties, and it really wasn't that cold. Because who can play in the snow and not drink hot chocolate afterwards, right?"

"Yeah. Exactly."

"Have you decided what tree you want?"

"I thought we were getting a blue spruce."

"I thought you said you didn't like them because they didn't last very long."

"And then we decided that we're going to get one because we're not keeping it up until Valentine's Day."

"All right. I didn't realize that that conversation had a conclusion, so, glad you were there to interpret for me."

"Oh my goodness. That's ridiculous. You heard everything I heard."

"I didn't come to that conclusion at all. I thought we're in the middle of talking about it when... We got distracted or something."

"What about that one?" she asked, pointing to a scraggly blue spruce that looked like it had been stunted for some reason.

"So we're getting a Charlie Brown tree?" he asked, tilting his head as though trying to figure out what in the world to say about it.

"It's cute."

"It's ugly."

"In a cute kind of way."

"It's ugly, and there's no way you can spin it to try to make it be cute too."

"Don't you feel bad for it?"

"Feel bad? Why would I feel bad?"

"I dunno. Because it doesn't look as nice as the other trees around it."

"But it's a tree. Trees don't have feelings."

"I know, but still, people are going to come, they're going to pick the trees around it, they're going to be very happy with those trees, and it's just going to be left here, and it's going to be sad."

"If trees do feel anything, which I still maintain that they can't, this tree would not feel sad, it would feel happy that it was still alive, not dead like all the other trees that look nicer. So actually, the fact that it's ugly will save its life."

"It will feel sad because all the other trees got to go home for Christmas and it didn't. And it will be sad all year, and maybe next year it'll hope that he can be pretty, but it just was never in the cards for it to look anything more than..."

"Ugly."

"Scraggly and cute."

They spoke at the same time, and turned twinkling eyes toward each other.

"If you want that tree, we can get it, but just don't ask me to sit and admire it and pretend that it looks anything other than —"

"Ugly. I know."

"So that's the one?" he asked, holding up a saw that he dug out of the shed knowing that it would be too early for them to get one from the Christmas tree farm.

"No. We're not going to get it if you don't like it. I feel bad for it because no one else is going to choose it either, but we need to get a tree that both of us agree on. Isn't that what marriage is supposed to be about? We compromise. I don't get my way all the time and you don't get yours."

"But if we don't get the tree, then I'm getting my way."

He tilted his head and looked at her as though he knew he was putting her in a pickle.

"I guess that's true. But there's no way we can cut down half a tree. So, I guess you just get your way this time. Because, at least I'm not making you look at an ugly tree from now until Christmas."

"It's not very long until Christmas, so it's not like it's two weeks before Thanksgiving and I'm going to have to look at it for the next six weeks."

"That's a good point."

"So do you want the tree?" he asked, taking a step toward it, the crunching of the snow the only sound other than the wind whistling through the tops of the trees.

"No. It has to be one we both like. Not just me."

He was right that he was kinda getting his way if they didn't get that tree, but she really didn't want to take a tree home that he didn't like. She wouldn't feel like she was getting her way at all. Not if her husband didn't like the tree."

Her husband. That was still so odd.

But it felt good, as they bantered with each other, the snow sparkling around them, the wind lifting her hair and blowing it across her face, and him reaching out to push it back. Maybe his finger lingered just a little on her cheek, maybe their eyes held for just a little longer, or maybe he felt the same oddly good twirling sensation in his stomach that she did.

Maybe not.

Maybe if he did he would do something about it, kiss her.

But he didn't make any move to do that and started walking again without looking at her.

"What kind of tree is your favorite?" he asked as he moved along.

"I like White Pine. They're pretty."

"They're not your favorite," he said that as a statement, and took two steps before he said, "Douglas Fir. That's your favorite."

"You're right. But, we don't have to get Douglas Fir. We can do that next year if we get our tree a little earlier."

"Maybe we'll have a house that actually has room for a tree next year," he said as he turned, heading toward the field with the Douglas fir in it.

"Jones. Let's get a blue spruce."

"I want a Douglas fir."

"And I want a blue spruce."

They stopped, and she put her hands on her hips. She wasn't going to allow him to not get a blue spruce just because she liked Douglas fir. It didn't always have to be what she wanted.

"You're the one who likes Christmas trees."

"You're the one who suggested we get one."

"But you're the one who wants the house to look like Christmas when we come home from the funeral."

"That's true I said that, but you're the one who suggested the tree in the first place."

"All right. We'll compromise." He nodded his head, and she narrowed her eyes, reading that look from a mile away. He had something tricky up his sleeve.

"All right," she said cautiously.

"Let's get a white pine."

A laugh burst out of her mouth. "Of course." She shook her head, still grinning. "That is so you."

"That didn't sound like a yes."

"Yes." His solution was perfect. She wanted to get the blue spruce for him, and he wanted to get the Douglas fir for her, and neither one of them wanted to get the one that they really wanted because they didn't want to not get what the other wanted, so his solution was hilarious and appropriate.

Neither one of them got what they wanted.

"We're sad people, aren't we?" he said as they turned and started walking toward the white pine.

"I'd say we're sweet, but I'm not even sure about that. After all, we kind of both just shot each other in the foot."

"We're ourselves, depending on how you look at it."

It didn't take long for them to pick out a white pine. They had it cut down and Patricia was in the office when they got to the parking lot, and they paid for their tree.

They had enough time to get it up before Amy's mom called, asking if they could come watch the kids so that she and Isadora could go somewhere and talk.

"I'm sorry my family has lumped you in with me as the go-to babysitter," Amy said as they took one last look at the white pine in their living room in their tiny little house, before they turned out the lights and walked out the door.

"What did we say earlier? That anything I do is better if I do it with you?"

"That doesn't mean you enjoy it."

"Then you can just say that you make anything I do enjoyable."

He stood looking at her and she glanced at him, and she wasn't quite sure what passed between them, but it felt warm and good and she nodded in agreement.

"And anything I do is more enjoyable when you're with me."

Chapter Twenty-Four

Jones stood by himself at the side of the church, watching as people milled about at the meal that had been provided for the family after the funeral.

The funeral had been sad, no doubt, and hard for Gilbert and the children. It had been hard for Amy's mom to watch too, Jones would've said. He couldn't imagine watching his child suffer like that.

But, Marjorie had been strong throughout all of it, and the pillar that her children could lean on.

The kids had gathered around him and Amy at times, and they also found comfort in Judd and Terry.

Isadora seemed to be dealing with her own issues, and had left halfway through when one of her children had not been able to sit still.

She had them in a high chair now, and was feeding one while an older lady from the church talked to her, although if Jones had to guess, Isadora wasn't paying much attention to what she was saying at all.

His parents hadn't shown up, not that he expected them to.

But, it had been hard for him to focus on what was going on around him. All he wanted to think about was how to get those confounded pillows out from between Amy and him at night.

"Hey there," Judd said, clamping a hand on his shoulder as he walked up to Jones. You found yourself a quiet corner, huh?"

"I guess. Sometimes it's nice to just stand back and take it in." And Amy had been grabbed by one of the ladies in the church who wanted her to do something for the Christmas Eve service.

He'd be spending Christmas Eve with Amy. Not like they had never spent Christmas Eve together before, but...it was different this year and he knew it.

"How's married life treating you?" Judd said, smiling some, as though he knew it was really good.

"Looks like you're enjoying it," Jones said, not wanting to say that he didn't seem to know how to move past friendship with his wife, and part of him was scared to.

"I am. I guess it wouldn't be nearly so enjoyable with the wrong woman, but I've got a wonderful one, and I certainly think the next fifty years are going to be pretty stinking good."

He only wished he felt that way. The next fifty years stretched out intolerably before him, a pillow always between Amy and he, or the other scenario, where he moved too fast and ruined what they had, and they ended up awkward and disliking each other.

"Yeah," he finally said, knowing he paused way too long.

"So... I guess I should admit that Terry wanted me to come over and say something to you."

Jones huffed out a laugh. That was just like Terry. She's been gone for a while, but he remembered her as a typical oldest child, always trying to control everything, and making sure her siblings were taken care of.

"Wonder why?" he said, just to give Judd an opening, since Judd wasn't exactly known for his great conversational skills. It was a testament to how much he loved his wife that he was even standing there to begin with.

"She's worried that you and Amy are having trouble figuring out how to be more than friends."

It was tempting for Jones to deny that, and he probably would have, or changed the subject or skirted around it, if it hadn't been Judd and Terry, Amy's beloved older sister.

"I love Amy, but I'm having some issues. I don't know that there's anything to be worried about, but... I just don't want to ruin what we have, you know? By forcing more than what she wants."

"You're not sure what she wants?"

"Yeah. Although we agreed that our marriage would be real, that we'd have children, I guess I just don't know what she wants right now."

"What do you want?"

"I want to get rid of the pillows."

Judd looked confused.

"She put pillows down the middle of the bed to make us both comfortable, that's what she said. I would be more comfortable without them."

"You don't like pillows?"

"No. It's what the pillows represent. It's a whole thing in my head now, that's between Amy and me. And, she's the one who wanted the pillows. So it makes me feel like she's not ready for more."

"Why don't you ask her?"

"Because that will make everything awkward. And Amy and I have such a great relationship, I don't want awkwardness."

"You and Amy have such a great relationship, do you think the awkwardness will last for the next fifty years? Like it might be awkward for a little bit if you want more than what she does, or, as Terry and I suspect, you both want the same thing, but both of you are scared to death of what you just said — ruining what you have.

And, you're not getting into the idea that what you have could be made even better by moving forward."

"Better?" Jones asked, lifting his brows. He couldn't imagine what he and Amy had being any better, although maybe intimacy would make it better. Or add another level to it.

"Is she selfish? Is she hard to get along with? Has she ever gotten upset with something you said, or over something stupid without taking into consideration your point of view?"

"No, no, no." He had needed someone to ask him those questions. "I guess I couldn't articulate that myself, but the picture just came into focus as you said that." He shrugged his shoulders. "It's silly for me to be sitting around wondering, when yeah, it's going to be awkward if we're not on the same page, but it's not going to last. And we're not going to get upset with each other. We agreed to this marriage, and both of us knew what it would mean going into it."

"Exactly." Judd grinned. "That was easier than I thought it was going to be." He paused and then he said, "We've been friends for so long, I was afraid that my question was going to make things awkward between us." It took a second before Jones realized that the usually taciturn Judd was teasing him.

"Shut up," he said, pushing him on the shoulder.

"Just go tell Amy you want to kiss her. Or, whatever else it is you want to do." Judd rolled his eyes and walked away, leaving Jones grinning stupidly behind him. Was it going to be that easy? Just tell her what he wanted?

He hadn't figured out how to say it before the funeral meal was over, and maybe that was a good thing, since a funeral wasn't the best place to bring up that conversation anyway.

When they got home, the tree didn't do much to cheer them up, since it was still not decorated.

"It was a nice idea," Amy said as she glanced at the tree, before turning to him. "Is it okay if I get a shower?"

"Sure." He nodded, wanting to ask, but finding his tongue stuck to the roof of his mouth. It was Amy; he could ask her anything. Except...apparently, whether or not she would be okay if he kissed her.

Plus, shouldn't a kiss have a romantic setting? Especially if it was going to be their first kiss.

He wasn't sure whether he was overthinking it, or not thinking about it enough, and he still hadn't figured that out by the time he was done with his shower.

But instead of coming out of the bathroom fully dressed, he came out with just a towel around his waist. Seeing Amy do a double take was more than worth the few moments of anxiety that doing that had induced in him.

She raised her brows, and then looked up at him, as though looking for answers to questions that she hadn't asked on his face.

He stood still a few feet away from the bed, and even though he knew that he was making way more out of this than he needed to, he swallowed hard, and then asked one of the hardest questions he'd ever had asking his life before. "I was hoping we could get rid of the pillows."

Stupid. He hadn't even kissed her. And he wanted to get rid of the pillows. She was going to say –

A pillow landed at his feet. On the heels of that one came another one.

"I didn't think you were ever going to ask."

Her eyes twinkled, and he realized that Judd was most likely right. They both had been thinking the same thing.

"I didn't want to make a move because I had determined in my heart that I would just follow your lead, and we would move forward when you were ready."

"And I had decided that you didn't really like me because you hadn't made any moves, and I wasn't going to make any move until you made a move because I didn't want you to have to be with someone you didn't really like that way."

"Oh, Amy," he said, walking to the bed and kneeling down beside it, running a hand over her hair and cupping her cheek.

Her hand came up and ran across his temple then down his shoulder.

"Don't think I wasn't nervous. I am still nervous."

"Don't be. It's just me."

I know, but it feels...different."

"It doesn't have to be. We don't have to do anything. Just...no pillows."

"I think I want to do more than no pillows. But, maybe we could start with kissing?" She looked around, and the hopeful look on her face made the corners of his mouth turn up.

"That's pretty much all I've been thinking about since our wedding night. How I can get you to kiss me."

"Tell me you want me to?" she said.

"But I didn't want you to if you didn't want to. It's like the tree, you know?"

Her hand wrapped around his neck, and she tugged gently.

"And, I thought that maybe I should have some kind of romantic setting. We should be gazing dreamily into each other's eyes under a starry sky or full moon or something like that."

His mouth got closer to hers, and their noses bumped together.

"Are you going to talk about it? Or are you going to actually focus on doing it?"

"You don't want some kind of romantic thing?"

"Is this not romantic?" she asked, sounding like she truly thought it was.

"To me, it's perfect."

"It's not perfect until your lips are on mine," she said, and she leaned forward just a bit, touching the corner of his mouth with hers.

"You missed," he said.

She giggled, and with that, it didn't feel awkward anymore, and he didn't know about her, but his nervousness fled away as well. It was Amy, and they would do what they always did. Laugh and have fun, even if it was kissing. Because, he couldn't imagine anything being better than kissing his best friend.

Then, as though to prove that she wasn't going to miss, her lips landed on his, and he knew, at that point for sure, that there truly wasn't anything better than kissing his best friend.

Chapter Twenty-Five

*A*my yawned and stretched, feeling good and happy clear down to her bones. She settled herself more firmly against Jones, throwing an arm over his chest, and smiling as his arm tightened around her, his hand resting on her hip.

The funeral had been hard, harder than she expected, mostly seeing the children and her mom, and the stoicism of her brother. It wasn't that she missed Sally so much, or was so sad to have her gone; it was more to see the pain of people she loved.

The disappointment that they hadn't gotten her tree decorated, and had come home to more of the same, had her down. But, Jones had flipped all that on its head when he had come out of the bathroom and tackled the thing that neither one of them wanted to talk about head on.

"I love you," she said, knowing it had been true for a long time. Sure, she hadn't seen Jones as husband material, but she had loved him forever.

"I love you too. I love you more. I love you forever."

His words made her smile, partly because she might have said it first, but he said it better. And partly because she didn't think she'd ever get tired of hearing him say that.

Her leg stretched out over his, and she turned her head, kissing his jawline.

"Thank you for saying something. Who knows how long we would have gone on before I finally found the courage to do it."

"I can't believe it took courage for you to talk to me about something like that. I don't understand."

"It took courage for you to talk to me."

"True. But I guess my fear was it would be awkward, but, don't hate me, but Judd talked to me a little bit at the funeral, and I realized that no matter what kind of an idiot I made out of myself, you never got mad at me, it's never been weird between us, and even if you do get upset, which you are human and you do, it wasn't going to be forever. We could work it out."

"So you told Judd that you and I hadn't —"

"No. We didn't talk about that. Not really. He just said that Terry was concerned about us, and sent him over because she thought we both had the same problem. Neither one of us wanted to ruin our friendship. And she just wanted us to be reminded that there was a reason that we'd been friends for so long."

"Because you're awesome, and who wouldn't want to be friends with you."

"No doofus," he said, kissing her forehead to take any sting out of his words, although it sounded more like an endearment when he said it. "It's that we work through things. We're good together. We get along, we... Yeah. It was better than I thought it was going to be. If that is even possible."

His voice faded off a little, almost as though he was in unfamiliar territory and wasn't quite sure how she was going to take that.

And it made every part of her body feel good.

"Really?" she asked, kissing his neck.

"No. Maybe we ought to do it again just to see if it's as good as what I remember."

"It wasn't that long ago," she said, but she wasn't going to argue with him. She was all on board with that suggestion. Not that she wouldn't be on board with all of his suggestions. Because marriage wouldn't be any fun if it was all about her, and she wasn't doing everything she could to encourage and uplift and be the best wife she could be to the man she married.

"Was that a no?" he asked, his fingers trailing along her hip.

"That was yes. Sorry I wasn't more clear. It was a yes, please, and I'll help you get started," she said, as her fingers moved along his abs.

"This could get interesting," he said, and she smiled. What she said, about everything being more fun with Jones, was absolutely true. She should have known that it would apply to everything.

Chapter Twenty-Six

"I don't think I'm going to be able to be the Secret Saint anymore." Wilson McBride stacked the last piece of wood he and Judd had delivered to a family who needed it and couldn't afford it for their stove.

"You're not?" Judd said, obviously surprised.

Wilson hated breaking it to him like this, but he'd been thinking about it for a while. He wanted to help as many people as he could, but more and more, he'd been thinking that maybe that wasn't the right approach. Or maybe he should say, it wasn't the approach that God wanted him to have.

"I think I need to go in a different direction."

"All right. I'm not going to try to stop you if that's what you think." Judd paused, throwing his last piece down, and dusting his gloves off. "I know you wouldn't be doing it without a lot of prayer and without feeling like your direction was coming from the Lord.

"Yeah. Although, what I'm thinking about is so crazy, I'm not sure I can justify it with anything."

"All right. Is it a secret?"

"I'm not telling too many people, but I figure I owe you an explanation."

"I'm listening," Judd said as they walked slowly back through the dark toward the truck. The family had been away for the day, and they weren't worried about anyone seeing them.

"When we first started this, I knew that I could do a little for a lot of people, versus doing a lot for just one person."

"Yeah. I can see that. There's just so much need, and it's hard to not want to spread everything around, but sometimes you feel like you're just putting Band-Aids on a gaping wound, and you're not making much of a difference."

"I felt like that a lot. And I wish there was more I could do, but if you focus on one person, then you feel like you're leaving others behind."

"Yes, only in my case...do you remember Charity Ames?"

"With the five kids. Her husband ran off with his girlfriend to Australia so that he didn't have to pay child support. Of course. Of course."

"I've been thinking about her a lot, and those kids, that poor woman, she's about to lose everything, and she's scared she's going lose her children, because she can't take care of their home and she's just had so much hardship... I know I can help her, but that means I'm going to have to give up helping everyone else."

"How are you going to help her?"

"I'm going to marry her."

Read _Sugarplum Dreams_, the next book from Mistletoe Meadows series featuring Wilson and Charity. When Wilson decides to do the

biggest good deed he's ever considered tackling, Charity and her five kids might just find their missing puzzle piece.

Sneak Peek of Sugarplum Dreams

"It's been nice doing the Secret Saint with you," Wilson said as he and Judd Landis finished packing the last Christmas tree onto the trailer where they were taking them to an assisted living facility where children were going to help decorate them on Christmas Eve.

"Same," Judd said as he tightened the strap holding the trees down on the small trailer. Then he straightened. "But I get it. You can't help Charity Ames as well as the Secret Saint as you can as her husband." He paused for a moment then tilted his head. The fading light bathed his face in shadows, and Wilson couldn't see the expression on it. "Did you even ask her if she would marry you?"

Wilson huffed out a laugh. "You know, I've never asked anyone to marry me before. And I can see how guys would get nervous asking someone they've dated for years. But I think that they would have a pretty good idea that she would say yes. For me, I have no idea what Charity is going to say. I've been...dragging my feet about it."

"So that that means...no?" Judd said, and Wilson didn't have any trouble seeing the gleam of his teeth despite descending darkness.

Wilson nodded. "Yeah. That means no." His grin was self-deprecating, although he doubted Judd could see his face any better than he could see his. Which was probably just as well. Judd couldn't see his hands shaking either.

He was trying to do a good deed, that was the thought behind asking Charity to marry him, but that didn't make him any less nervous.

"So if she says no... I'm not losing my partner?"

"No. Although, it might take a little bit before I'm able to talk about it."

"That's okay. We're pretty much done for this year. I suppose I'll have figured out by next year if you and Charity don't get married."

"That would be a pretty big hint." He never even thought about a marriage of convenience until he started this Secret Saint thing, where he and Judd had been helping the more unfortunate members of their little town of Mistletoe Meadows, set high in the Blue Ridge Mountains of central Virginia. But Charity's husband had run off with his girlfriend, leaving her to take care of their five children and a boatload of debt. Charity was drowning, and even though the town had rallied to help her, she was afraid that she was going to be losing her children, if anyone figured out that she wasn't able to take care of them. She confided as much to Wilson, and he wished at the time that there was more he could do.

Marrying her was more than most people would do, but... It seemed like the perfect solution. At least from his end. Maybe Charity wouldn't think so.

He could see a lot of issues, could hear a lot of arguments in his head. Maybe that was why he hadn't talked about it to too many people. He didn't have a choice about talking to Judd about it though, since he wouldn't be doing the Secret Saint anymore, and Judd had a right to know.

"I actually have someone in mind to replace you, if this thing with Charity goes through."

"I had a couple of names swirling around in my head too, but if you've got someone, then you don't need my suggestions." His brother Roland seemed like a good idea. He wasn't married and had a heart of gold, although he seemed a little gruff on the edges. He definitely wouldn't go around blabbing about it.

"I'm open to suggestions," Judd said as he leaned against the side of the truck, looking up at the darkening sky as the stars started popping out.

"It's probably better that I don't have any clue who you decide to choose. It was fun being anonymous. But it did seem like the more people who found out, the more the town knew, the less we were able to do."

"There is a certain freedom that is granted in anonymity," Judd concurred, not the slightest bit offended that Wilson was going to keep his names to himself. As much as he'd love to see his brother get into it, if Judd was going to carry it on, he deserved to choose the person he felt was best for the role.

"I'm glad you're going to continue though. I was kind of upset about the idea of there being no more Secret Saint. And I know the town will be disappointed."

"I might have to quit eventually. I'm married, but we don't have five children. Not yet."

"So how's married life treating you?" Wilson asked, knowing that Judd had just gotten married a couple of weeks ago to Wilson's oldest sister, Terry.

Judd nodded, and a sappy grin that even the weak light couldn't hide split his face. "It's good."

That was all he said, but his tone and his expression spoke far more. Judd was very happy.

"I'd suggest you wait until you find the right person, but I have a feeling that Terry is one of a kind, and no matter how long you wait or how hard you search, you'll never find anyone as good as her."

"I think that's the way a man's supposed to feel about his wife. I know that's the way Terry feels about you."

Judd grinned. But it was true. Even though Terry and Judd didn't really know each other before Terry had moved back to Mistletoe

Meadows to open up her medical practice, and they fell in love quickly, they were just as happy as Amy and Jones who had been friends forever and just realized that they were in love.

Wilson had been just a little bit jealous that Amy and Terry had gotten married on the same day, finding their perfect matches and beginning a life together full of love and joy and happiness.

At the wedding, Wilson had pretty much already decided that he was going to propose to Charity. He wasn't under the impression that it was going to be a love match. Although he had debated about whether or not he should try to court Charity rather than just propose a marriage of convenience which did not sound the slightest bit romantic.

He figured that Charity wasn't interested in a man's attentions, not after what her husband had done to her, and he doubted she was very interested in romance either.

But he didn't know very much about women, not any more than what he learned growing up with sisters and through the few failed relationships that he had in his late teens and early twenties.

"All right then, this is it. It's been fun. And while I don't wish that you get turned down, I won't be sad if we pick up the Secret Saint again next fall."

He grabbed Judd's outstretched hand and gave it a firm shake. "Same. I couldn't have worked with a better man. You have a vision and an ability to seem to be able to do exactly what the Lord wants you to. I've admired it, as well as the upright way you live your life. You're definitely a role model." He didn't usually get all sappy and complimentary, especially with another man, but it was true. Judd had taught him quite a bit in the last couple of years that they worked together. It was interesting to him the way Judd had followed the Lord, and God blessed him not just monetarily, but by bringing Terry into his life too. He didn't think he'd ever seen Judd so happy. In fact, he was sure of it.

Judd slapped him on the back and then walked to the front of the truck, got in the driver's side, and started the engine. Wilson stepped back and watched as Judd pulled out. It was just two days until Christmas, and it was past time that he do what he knew he was supposed to do but had been dreading.

Lord, this is such a crazy idea, I know it has to come from You. I don't know why I'm nervous. If I'm doing what You want me to do, it shouldn't matter whether she says yes or no. But I guess my pride is involved more than I want to admit. It would be a bit of a blow if she said no. But I can't quite bring myself to pray that she'll say yes. I guess, I just need to trust You and know that Your will will be done.

He could always talk to God and say whatever was in his heart. And somehow, just talking to the Lord and letting Him know that and reiterating that he was going to do whatever God wanted him to do calmed him more than anything else could. Not that his hands weren't still shaking, and not that his stomach didn't feel like it was being squeezed by a giant hand, but just that he knew that whatever happened, God was in control. And that was enough for him.

Sign up for Jessie's newsletter! Get a free book, access to exclusive bonus content, get fun and funny updates on her life on the farm and more!

A Gift from Jessie

Claim your free book from Jessie!

Escape to more faith-filled romance series
by Jessie Gussman!

The Complete Sweet Water, North Dakota Reading Order:

Series One: Sweet Water Ranch Western Cowboy Romance (11 book series)

Series Two: Coming Home to North Dakota (12 book series)

Series Three: Flyboys of Sweet Briar Ranch in North Dakota (13 book series)

Series Four: Sweet View Ranch Western Cowboy Romance (10 book series)

Spinoffs and More! Additional Series You'll Love:

Jessie's First Series: Sweet Haven Farm (4 book series)

Small-Town Romance: The Baxter Boys (5 book series)

Bad-Boy Sweet Romance: Richmond Rebels Sweet Romance (3 book series)

Sweet Water Spinoff: Cowboy Crossing (9 book series)

Small Town Romantic Comedy: Good Grief, Idaho (5 book series)

True Stories from Jessie's Farm: Stories from Jessie Gussman's Newsletter (3 book series)

Reader-Favorite! Sweet Beach Romance: Blueberry Beach (8 book series)

Blueberry Beach Spinoff: Strawberry Sands (10 book series)

From Strawberry Sands to: Raspberry Ridge (12 book series)

Swoonfully Jolly Holiday Stories:

Holiday Romance: Cowboy Mountain Christmas (6 book series)

Cowboy Mountain Christmas Spinoff: A Heartland Cowboy Christmas (9 book series)

New and Much Loved: Mistletoe Meadows (4 books and counting!)

Laughing Through the Snow: Christmas Tree, PA Sweet Romcoms (6 short reads)

9 7 9 8 8 9 3 8 2 1 2 3 9